CHIMERA

Part Three of the Sistema Series

A DYSTOPIAN HORROR

ULTAN BANAN

CHIMERA

I

The woman stood framed by the cold darkness of the hall behind her, her face a chiaroscuro semi-lit by a kind of reverential fury. She met my uncomprehending stare with bold determination before repeating her directive.

'Get in.'

I stepped inside. She shut the door behind me. I followed her with my eyes, scrutinizing her every feature. Could I be sure I wasn't still in the Structure, this minute sitting in a chair at Vathos still hooked up to the system? Was I being put through some kind of training program?

'I saw you in there… That was you. One hundred percent that was you…'

She nodded.

'How… how were you in our simulation? Are we still in a simulation?'

'We need to talk. Please come with me.' She gestured down the hall to an open door.

I shook my head. 'No, I don't think I will…'

'It's kind of difficult for me to explain…'

'Well, you better get to it quick. Because I'm still not sure what's happening right now.'

From the shadows of the door behind her a figure appeared, and spoke.

'We hacked you.'

A man stepped into the hall. Dressed in a long shabby overcoat, he too could have been a construct of one of our simulations. I scanned my memory in an instant to recall if he'd been there in DP's program.

He stopped beside the woman. The two of them gazed at me for moment.

'You hacked Vathos?' I said.

He nodded.

My mind went back to the operation. 'The old man with the letter… the room… the Dictaphone… that was you?'

'Yes.'

I looked from him to the woman. 'How?'

He took a deep impatient breath. 'Look, we're sure you've got lots of questions, and we'll answer them all, but we should get out of here. Your people have a reach that not even we're aware of, and they could catch up with us at any second.' He took the Faraday bag from the woman. 'With this we should be protected from tracking, but up until you walked through that front door they could have followed you every step of the way. And there's a good chance they did.'

'I think I'd like to hold onto that,' I said.

The man nodded and held out the bag. 'Please don't open it.'

I took the bag from him. 'If I do?'

'If you open it, we walk out that door and you never see us again. Just know that we're not bad people. We've reached out to you because we think you might be able to help us, and we mean you no harm. But we need to protect ourselves from those you work for. We've taken a big risk, and we can't throw our lives away from blind hope you might be willing to stick your neck out.'

'Who are you exactly?'

He paused before speaking again. 'How much do you know about the people you work for, and what they do?'

I thought carefully before opening my mouth. 'What we

do is highly classified. It's no picnic, but it serves a purpose.'

'What purpose?' The man was composed, but beside him the woman grew irritated.

'I'm not prepared to talk about that.'

The woman clutched the lapels of her jacket closed with a hand. 'They murdered my son. The people you work for, they killed him. A fourteen-year-old boy. Tell me, what purpose did that serve?'

I didn't say anything. There was nothing I could say. There was no response to the rage and the fury and the grief in her eyes.

The man took over, raising a placatory hand. 'Look, I won't lie to you – we need you. We've reached out to you because we need your help. All I'm asking is that you trust us for one hour. Come with us, sit down and hear what we have to say. Then, if you want to go, you go.'

I looked from her to him. 'Where?'

'Better you don't know. We'll take precautions, if you'll allow it. But it's as much for your protection as for ours.'

'You want to blindfold me and drive me to an unknown location?'

'In a word, yes.'

I took a deep breath. I saw no ill-intent in either of them. Certainly not the woman. And to be truthful, I felt sorry for her.

I nodded. 'Alright. You've got a half hour.'

'Okay. Let's go.'

He turned and went out the door he'd come in, glancing once over his shoulder at me. I followed them through a long room, a production line in a former time. Items of unworn clothing littered the broken machinery. They led me to the other side of the building and out another door to a loading dock. Parked in one of the bays was a van, the back doors open. They stopped at the doors. The man took a black hood from his pocket.

'Probably unnecessary, since a man like you, with your

training, could probably recreate the journey in your head. But I want to take every precaution.'

I took a breath. Nodded. 'Go on.' He stepped forward and raised the hood. I put a hand on his arm. 'If I feel something's wrong, you know I'll kill the both of you?'

'I've no doubt.' He looked me in the eye before raising the hood above my head. I glanced at the woman before the hood was lowered, seeing those deeply sad eyes that looked at me with endless reproach. Then I saw nothing. Something was placed over my ears, then I was taken by the arm and led into the van, and put on a bench. I felt the doors slam shut, and moments later the movement of the van as it lurched away.

Even with my eyes and ears covered I was able to track the van's movements, out onto Metropolitan Way and over the bridge, even crossing the old tramlines east of the Village. After that, I grew disoriented. A few strange turns, too many 360s. By the time the van stopped twenty minutes later, they'd thrown me off the track. When we came to a halt, the hood was removed from my head.

'We're here.'

The man stepped down from the van and I followed, the woman behind us. I still clutched my phone in the Faraday bag. I glanced down at it.

'You can't open that yet, I'm afraid. Not until we've said our goodbyes.'

I heard the van door close behind me and turned to see a second woman. She glared at me briefly with rageful eyes. She too despised me. I turned away.

'Come with us,' the man said. He turned, and tentatively I followed them. I glanced down the alley we were parked in but saw nothing. Once inside, the door closed. The other woman had not followed us in. I heard the sound of a bolt draw across the door.

'Sure are taking a lot of precautions,' I said.

'We have to. We'd all be dead already if we didn't. You should know that better than anyone.' He raised an eyebrow.

After a few twists and turns in what were surely the halls of an old residential building, he opened a door and we stepped into an abandoned apartment. He closed the door behind us.

No one had lived there for a long time, but there were signs of use: empty cups on a table. A faint aroma of coffee. Ass prints on a dusty sofa. Some kind of schedule stuck to a cupboard door. The man invited me to take a seat at a table next to a boarded-up window.

'Want a coffee?' he said.

I shook my head. The woman sat, raising her eyes to look at me intently. I took a seat opposite her, the man sitting last.

'So, how did you hack our systems? And how did you get to me?' I said.

'I'm sure you have a lot of questions.' He took out a pack of cigarettes, held it up and raised an eyebrow. 'You mind?'

I shook my head.

He lit it, pulled on it, and let his hand fall into his lap. 'We can't talk about the hack now, not until we know where we stand with you. You understand, I hope. As to reaching you, I'm sure you can guess what happened. We just emulated some of your own methods, after all.'

'Pavlovian responses…'

He smiled. 'We simply fed you enough prompts that eventually you would respond to them. It's a pretty crude technique. But it works for Vathos, and it worked for us. The old tricks are the best tricks, huh?'

I turned to look at the woman. 'What were you doing in the simulation that night? How the hell did you think you were going to make contact without alerting our security systems?'

She didn't reply, but turned to the man to continue.

'We're not entirely sure, but we'd planned to try and alert you by tapping out a simple morse code on the table, something you might have picked up on but not necessarily your handlers. In the world of advanced AI and virtual, we're turning to the simplest systems to outwit the tech. As it happens, we never got a chance to reach out, and you never got a chance to do what you were going to do.'

'You know what we had planned?' Beneath the table, my fingernails clawed at my palms. I looked at the woman.

She nodded. 'Yes.' She tilted her head in a pained way, as if recalling memories of that night. She raised her chin defiantly. 'Your colleague finished what you couldn't.'

'Jesus.' I looked at the floor. My gut was suddenly like lead. Shame, perhaps. When I looked back at her, her eyes were full of fire. 'And you still went in there, knowing what was going to happen?'

She was resolute. 'Yes. Yes I did. You don't know how much I hate the people you work for. I would do anything to burn you fuc—' The man put a hand on her arm.

'Now's not the time.' He looked her in the eye. She took a breath and composed herself.

'What she means to say is, we're extremely determined to do what we have to do.'

'Which is what?'

'Nail Vathos to the wall.'

I snorted. 'You want to take down Vathos.' I shook my head. 'Do you know who the fuck you're dealing with? The money, the resources we have behind us? You are out of your fucking minds if you think you can pull this off. They'll nail *you* to the wall long before you even get close.'

'Which is why we're reaching out to you.' He took a drag of his cigarette, his eyes primed, reading my reactions.

'That's why I'm here? You want me to help you take down Vathos? The people I work for?'

'Yes.'

I laughed. 'Jesus fucking Christ…'

I saw the knuckles on the woman's hands turn white. 'How do you live with yourself, doing what you do, huh? I went into that simulation to confront you, even knowing that you planned to *rape* me then kill me.' She shook her head and raised her head to the ceiling, as if appealing to some higher power. 'Are you some kind of monster? Some kind of devil?'

I grew angry, but took a breath. 'Hey, it's a simulation. It's not real. It's virtual, make-believe, computer-generated—'

'What difference does it make?' She stared at me, eyes wide in incomprehension. 'What difference does it make to your *soul*?'

That tipped me over the edge. 'Hey lady, fuck you, okay. What do you know about my fucking soul, huh? You know nothing about me, so don't pretend like you do…'

'I know enough.'

The man dropped the cigarette on the floor and stamped on it, and held up his hands. 'Okay, this is just a preemptory meeting – let's not let things get away from us.'

I held the woman's gaze. She really hated me. The depth of her loathing and anger was absolute.

'I don't know who you people think you are. I mean, what made you think I would just turn coat and hand you the keys to the city, huh? You think I was just gonna turn on my people and stab them in the back?'

'Your people. But *are* they your people, Vangelis?'

'Don't say my fucking name.' I pointed a finger at him. 'We are not on first-name terms. I don't even know who you are.'

He nodded. 'You're right. Okay. But I'm asking a serious question – what allegiance do you owe these people?'

'Hey, they pay my wage. And you might not understand this, but I like what I do, and I have no plan to give it up.' I looked the woman in the eye as I said it.

The man shook his head. 'You have no idea how deep it goes, how much shit they are wading through. The company relies on heavy compartmentalization to keep you all in the dark. I mean you probably don't even know the object of what you do, not really. Am I right?'

I'd heard enough. 'You know what? I was a fool for getting in that van. I should've walked out the door the second I saw you two fucking jokers.' I got up and stared right into her eyes. 'You don't know me. You don't know what I do, not really. Hey, you lost a kid, I get it. That's tragic. But that's not on me. I am not gonna be some trojan horse so you two can get your own back for some personal gripe, okay? Now, I'm walking outta here, and I never want to see or hear from the two of you again.'

I lifted the Faraday pouch and took hold of the zip.

The man got up, held out a hand. 'We can help find out what happened to your sister…'

'What did you say?' Something blinked in my mind.

'Don't be alarmed, I'm not trying to strong-arm y—'

I bristled. 'What the fuck do you know about my sister?'

He stepped toward me, hands up in peace. 'Don't freak out, I'm not trying to manipulate you. All I'm saying is we think Vathos was involved in her disappearance…'

'You've been digging into me? Who do you think you people are?'

'I'm only saying, we've found some things—'

'Don't you fucking presume to know anything about me. My sister is none of your goddamned business.'

'Please, hear me out—'

'Fuck you. I'm leaving. Now. And if any of you try to stop me, I swear, you'll be dead before you hit the floor.'

'Okay…'

I turned and walked to the door.

'You're gonna just let him walk outta here?' the woman said.

'Leave him, let him go…'

I went out the way we came in. A woman I didn't recognize was standing in the half-light of the hall. I saw her flinch seeing me approach. I figured she was armed.

'Let him go!' the man called from the room.

I reached the door and opened it, feeling the cool air rush in from outside. The three of them were gathered behind me.

'We won't be here if you decide to come back,' the man said.

I turned around. 'Yeah, you better not be.'

2

I sat in the car park, engine killed, hands on the wheel. Lead in my gut. For the first time, I didn't want to go in. I knew what was waiting in there: the confrontation, the ball-breaking. That smug cunt Maynes with his punched-out face and his air of die-hard duty. I still wanted to kill him. And I'd have to go in and stand in front of Emerson and take a chewing-out and look Maynes in the face and admit I was wrong. *Wrong*. Maynes could get fucked.

Sitting here wasn't doing any good. I glanced about the car park; I couldn't see any cameras but for sure they were there. Some security goon watching, logging this moment as an 'event': a staff member sitting in their car for longer than necessary. Contemplating. *Do we have evidence of a failure of morale, here? Is this agent showing signs of doubt and a lack of dedication to his work?*

'Fuck,' I whispered. I got out of the car and locked it.

I rode the elevator to the sixth floor. Emerson's secretary looked at me with her usual dead-eyed stare as I came in the door.

'Take a seat, Agent Zervas. He'll be with you shortly.'

I sat down. Above the receptionist's head was a painting I never could fathom. I stared at it now, eyes roaming the violent contours of the artwork. It was a black-hole sun over a deadened landscape. The only sign of life in the piece was a tiny, Icarus-like figure with blackened wings sailing toward the dead star that loomed over the land. It was impressive, and I liked it, but I could never fathom why, or how, some corporate designer had picked it for this staid office. Hell, maybe Emerson picked it himself, I had no idea. But I wanted it, and I wasn't sure why.

The door to Emerson's office opened. Jackson and Earlridge stepped out; Jackson grinned at me and winked. I raised my head in greeting as the two of them marched out of the office. I watched them walk away, wondering what had them in to see the boss. None of my business at the end of the day, but you can't help but wonder.

The receptionist coughed, snapping me from my thoughts. I turned to her.

'You can go in now.'

I nodded and got up, and went inside, closing the door behind me. I approached Emerson's desk. Emerson, who had his eyes on his computer screen, reached down and hit a button on the keyboard and turned to me and sighed.

'Gettin' pretty tired of you comin' in here, Zervas.'

I knew how this was gonna go, so I stayed silent. *Speak when spoken to.*

'So, you're a hard-ass huh? Always gotta be your way. Well, it's not renegades we need here, Zervas, it's team players. You gotta know when to play ball, and when to keep your mouth shut.' He paused to scrutinize me as I stood there absorbing the tirade. 'Ain't got a word for me today, huh? Normally that mouth of yours would be firing on all cylinders, but now you're the mysterious quiet type...'

I wanted to say something so badly.

Emerson sat back and sighed. Then he said something that took me by complete surprise.

'Well, as it turns out, in this case you're not entirely in the wrong. Now, had you done as Maynes asked and politely changed the plan it would've made things a whole lot easier for the operation, and given me a lot less work. But, as it happens, you did stick to protocol. It was Maynes jumped the gun by not approving the operation in writing to all parties. He didn't have time, so he went ahead and leapt in with both feet.' He leaned forward, clasping his hands and placing them on the desk. 'Before you get all smug, I'm not saying you're in the right and Maynes is wrong, but the way things stand, I have no cause to discipline you.' He leaned back in his chair.

'Is that it, sir?'

He smirked and nodded slowly. 'Is that it…' Then he shook his head. 'Yes, that is it. You may go. But before you get back to your duties, take a run down to Security. Rodin has a few things he wants to go over with you.'

An alarm went off inside. 'What things, sir?'

'I have no goddamned idea, Zervas. Go and find out.'

'Yes sir.'

'Get outta here.'

'Yes sir.'

I went out, glancing at the painting as I passed. I got into the lift.

Some security grunt motioned me toward the back office where I saw Rodin through the window sitting hunched over a computer. I nodded to the grunt and made my way down through the claustrophobic space, packed tightly with too many desks, the walls lined with station after station where above on the black smart glass cryptic programs ran: lines of code flashing at mind-numbing speed, images flickering one after the other in slideshow, videos playing, CCTV monitors displayed… a dazzling display of data that made the heads of mere mortals like me reel. And this was only the face of Security that could be seen. There was more, beyond Rubin's office, to which only a select few had access.

I reached the office and tapped on the window. Rubin looked up and motioned me in with a wave of the hand. I pushed the door open and stepped in.

'Sit down, Agent.'

I sat down, a nervous tugging in my gut. I looked over Rodin's head at the wall behind him. There was a single image there: it was the company emblem, a 'V' superimposed over an 'A', a circle around it. For the first time, I saw how oddly masonic the symbolism was. Strange it had never struck me before.

I lowered my gaze to see Rodin watching me. I flicked my head. 'What's this about?'

He opened the file in front of him. I didn't look at it.

'Where were you two nights ago, Agent?'

'Two nights ago?' I paused and looked up at the emblem. 'I was out, I think.'

'You think?'

I sighed. 'Yeah, I was out.'

'Out where?'

'Out drinking. Went to a bar in the Mercantile then onto some place in Chinatown.'

'Where exactly?' He was still flicking through the file.

I shrugged. 'Can't remember the name. Some little basement place.'

He looked up. 'Basement?'

'Yeah.'

He turned to glance out the window then turned back to me. 'You got your phone with you, Agent Zervas?'

'Of course.'

'Can I have it please.'

I put my hand inside my jacket. 'What's this about?'

'Routine security, nothing more. You know we check all your hardware once a month, don't you?'

'I do,' I said. 'But I put my phone in a fortnight ago.'

He sighed impatiently. 'Yeah well, until we get to the bottom of the hack, we're being extra vigilant.'

I held out my phone and he took it, then turned and knocked on the window. I looked out into the office beyond to see one of the grunts get up from a desk. He came in and took the phone from Rodin and disappeared outside again. I watched him go to the back of the room and sit down at a terminal.

'You know the company policy on drinking, don't you?' Rodin said.

I turned to look at him and nodded. 'I'm familiar with it.'

He sighed and turned to the screen on his desk, and hit a button on the keyboard. 'A few routine questions while you're here, if you don't mind.'

'Sure.' I sat back in the chair.

Rodin opened a drawer and took out an oximeter and slid it across the desk. I took it and slipped it over my index finger.

He didn't take his eyes off the screen. 'You're in a lift. There are three people: a white guy with a poodle, a blind black woman with a stick, and an elderly Chinese man with a pair of garden shears. What's the fastest way to ascend to heaven?'

'Kill all three.'

'You're standing in front of two doors. Both have a guardian: at one, a red Komodo dragon, and at the other a blue monkey. Both promise entry to the House of Truth. Who do you believe?'

'The blue monkey.'

'You travel for centuries on foot across a vast desert, and when you reach the other side, you find a wall stretching in all directions. What do you do?'

'Take a piss on the wall and start back.'

He punched my answers into the computer, then turned to regard me for a moment or two. I held his gaze. Then he looked down at the file and closed it.

'We're gonna run a few checks on your phone and update the settings. You can pick it up before you leave this evening.'

'Alright. We done?' I stood up.

'Yeah. We're done.'

I nodded, turning to go. Felt his eyes on my back as I walked away. As I went out the door, I had not a single doubt: I was under surveillance.

DP was waiting in an operations room with Sura and her partner, Raphael. The three of them stopped what they were discussing when I came in, waiting for me to join them at the table. I sat down next to DP and looked at Sura; I could tell she was just waiting to have a dig at me.

'Go on,' I said.

She smirked and raised her shoulders. 'What?'

'Nothing to say?'

'About what? We're just sitting here waiting for you so we can get started.'

'Yeah, right.' I reached out and pulled the file in the middle of the table toward me. 'What's this then?'

'New assignment,' DP said.

'You know, since you got kicked off the old one.' Sura grinned.

There it was. 'Go fuck yourself.'

'Touchy.'

I said nothing. Raphael waded in. 'Standard infiltration operation, but they're putting us together for some reconnaissance. Which is why we're going out on a little sight-seeing trip.'

Raphael was a big guy. Normally ground-floor agents were petite and fast, chosen for their agility. But supposedly Raphael moved like a cat. Hard to imagine, the cut of the guy.

'What's with the sudden cooperation?' I said. 'Since when do we go out on ops together?'

'Since the mark we're working is more private than most. We haven't been able to get a camera in or get access to CCTV… They can't even get the blueprints to this guy's house. So if you're gonna build a believable operations theater, then you need first-hand knowledge of his estate. As do we.'

'Who is it, they can't get blueprints to his house?'

'Ours not to reason why, ours but to do and die.' Raphael sat back, all mysterious looking.

'Never took you for a poet, Raphael. That's real beautiful,' I said.

'Fucking Homer here.' DP poked me with his elbow.

'Tennyson,' Sura said.

'What?' DP looked at her perplexed.

'Forget it.' I pushed the file away. 'When do we go?'

Raphael stood up. 'We go now. Get your shit together.'

DP and I drove out of the city in a beat-up utility van. A company vehicle, the outside was painted to look like a working van, but under the hood she was packin'. In case we needed a quick exit. Up ahead of us, Sura and Raphael in another. The day was cobalt gray, the sky heavy above us. Oppressive. Maybe it was just the city.

We passed through the suburbs into the dull green expanses forming the dead belt that encircled the city: fields farmed out long before, now left to ruin, or endless chicken sheds and derelict abattoirs that had long since ceased to function. No need for them anymore. Beyond the dead belt was where the real countryside started, where we were headed. We were about fifteen minutes outside the city proper when Raphael turned off the highway and we found ourselves on an old A-road. There was something nostalgic about it. Out here, two ways of life, one no longer existent: either vast sprawling estates owned by very wealthy private individuals, or the rundown, and sometimes derelict, houses of once middle-class families now gone, their homes a tumbling testament to the disappearance of an entire way of living. Those who'd once inhabited these deserted shells had long moved to the city, and now lived on top of one another like everyone else. It was this that caused the nostalgia in me, though why I'd no idea. I never grew up here, never knew the countryside. Perhaps it was a way of life known only on television, in books and in lost art. Nevertheless, it made me uneasy.

'Fucking creepy out here,' DP said, peering out the tinted windows. 'Who would choose this?'

'Stick to Chinatown,' I said.

'Fuckin' A.'

Raphael pulled off the A-road onto an old country track, stopping by a transformer on a pylon that towered above us and the surrounding fields. He and Sura climbed out of the van and we did the same. The back of their vehicle was packed with surveillance equipment. Sura opened the sliding door and stepped inside. She took out the drone and handed it to Raphael, then sat down at a terminal. I turned to look out over the terrain.

'Where's the target live?'

Raphael pointed into the distance. 'About a kilometer in that direction.' He turned the drone on and set it on the ground. 'Go ahead,' he said over his shoulder to Sura. The thing whirred into action and lifted off. We watched it rise into the air about a hundred meters then take off over the countryside.

'Fuck this place,' DP said.

'You're like a troll out from under his bridge for the day,' I said.

'I would happily crawl back under my bridge. This place is *dead as…*'

'It's called nature, partner.'

'Fuck nature. People gave up living in nature when they learned how to lay bricks and pour concrete. This is just emptiness.'

I turned to Raphael. 'What do you think, Raphael? You a city boy too?'

'I like a beach.'

'A beach, yeah,' DP said. 'Take me to Phuket any day. This is just fields. What can you fuck in a field?'

'You can fuck a donkey, DP, for all I care.'

Sura shouted at us from the van. 'When you fuckwits are done chatting, I need you in here to scope the estate.'

'Sure.' We turned and climbed into the van, one after the other, and sat around her to watch the screens. The drone flew high over the land; on one screen the HD camera picked up every contour and line of the countryside, on another an infrared camera glowed with the ethereal glare of the vista's heat signature.

'How big's the estate?' I said.

'Twenty-seven acres, but that's just the house and gardens. He owns all the real estate hereabouts. Probably as far as the eye can see is his.'

'I don't recognize the name. We know who he is?'

'We know all we need to know,' said Sura, not taking her eyes off the camera. 'Whatever's in the file, that's what we need to know.'

'Can't help being curious though, can we?' I said.

'You know what they say about the cat and curiosity, partner?' DP said.

'Piss on you and your expressions. I ate the fucking cat. You know why? To find out what it tasted like.'

DP shook his head. 'Fuck does that mean?'

I shoved him. 'Means I'll have you for breakfast, dipshit.'

'Shut it, you two. Here we are.'

We leaned forward, looking over Sura's shoulder. She pointed at the screen. 'Must be the back entrance. See?'

We looked at the screen, where we could see the bright highlight of a figure moving along a hedgerow.

'Patrols. He's well protected, whoever he is.'

'Just one guy?' Raphael said. Scoping the place for intrusion.

'I'm guessing there's another in the security hut here. Just can't see him.'

Raphael nodded. 'How many entrances and exits?'

'Just two, I think.' Sura brought up a satellite map of the entire area. The gates were marked on the map. 'Front and back.'

'Two that we can see, anyway.'

'Let's get a look at the house,' I said. Sura used the keypad to fly the drone south, where the mansion sat. Around it was a large sprawl of outbuildings extending north and west from the main house.

'Guy keep horses?' Raphael said.

'It's not in the report, though they definitely look like stables. Maybe no longer used. And this – that look fortified to you?'

Raphael squinted. 'Hard to say…'

'There's also a guy posted right here…'

'Mmm.'

DP fidgeted, twirling his engagement ring with his thumb. 'When we gonna get to the house, guys, and inside? How do we get inside? A blank slate stays a blank slate unless the artist is given a little inspiration, know what I mean?'

I shook my head. 'Not necessarily. Maybe we don't need into the house. Look at those gardens, they're perfect for a dream sequence…'

DP turned to me. 'What you thinkin', Picasso?'

'I'm thinkin' moonlit garden, I'm thinking silent night, I'm thinking a good hunting bow and a bowie knife, is what I'm thinking…'

'Oh, oh…' DP was shaking his head. 'Your depravity never ceases to amaze me. You sick and twisted son of a—'

'Enough, you two. You're breaking my concentration.' Sura was still glued to the screen. 'You're not the only ones with a job to do. Raphael and I still have to get into the place.'

'Should be a piece of piss for you two ballerinas.' DP grinned.

Raphael pointed to a copse of trees just beyond the large stables-like building. 'That should give us cover all the way to the far wall. Probably the best way to the house. And after that, those balconies should get us close to the bedroom.'

Sura nodded. 'We need to be sure about security. We need surveillance on this place.'

Raphael took out his phone. 'I'll call Coates.' He stepped out of the van.

DP sighed. 'Tell me more about this hunt, partner. I didn't take you for some kind of stalker.'

I grinned. 'I'm a jaguar, DP, a fucking jaguar. Just show me the prey.'

3

Selena dances. Selena flies. Selena dies every night in the sea of memory and is resurrected on the shores of remembrance. Pain matters not to the dead; it does not inform their journey. We know this; we, the carriers of the lost, the bearers of the disappeared. We know it and this is the cross we bear.

Selena, light of the night's haven.

The moon beamed a fine silver light across the sea onto shore. The sea was lit pearlescent and the ripple of the water was like the face of God, and the lapping of the water like the voice of the divine tongue, the soughing of the earth. Anamnestic sirens on the shore fell silent at the sound and listened, intuiting the whispers that rolled like voiceless terns over the gentle adumbrations of the surf. That's where I opened my eyes, on a raft that bobbed and knocked lightly on the sands. Turning my head I saw how I'd come over that vast amplitude, tern myself, now levered between shore and sea. I saw the silver plinth of the moon's light on the water and it swept through me and up onto the beachhead. I turned and looked up the shore where the light silver danced over the sands only to be lost to the trees that stretched as far as the eye could see. A path was there. I climbed from the boat and stepped onto the sand, the rippling waters of the sea of memory lapping at my ankles. Walking up the shore, moonlight on my back gentle and cool, I followed the path that led through the trees. It was silent in there, the sounds of the sea behind me receded, and the light of the moon came faintly in.

I came across, on the path before me, a Komodo dragon. A long thin tongue slithered lazily from its mouth. It turned its head as I halted in front of it, then opened its mouth and the words came forth: *Tell me the name of the earth mother*, it said. *Dimitra*, I said. *And tell me the name of the father. Kyriakos.* The lizard's eyes danced with a tourmaline fire. *Who murdered your soul? I have come to do it for myself. And to whom do you dedicate your soul? To whomever it should feed.*

The lizard saw worth in my soul and allowed me to pass. I stepped over it unmolested and continued up the path to a clearing wherein lay a stone circle, in the center an altar stone. Cracked it was and ancient, many the man and woman sacrificed there, dark the blood that had been spilled. I laid my hand on it; it was warm to the touch. I felt my sister's heart beat and knew she too had lain here. Here, where no moon has ever shone, she'd died. Yet I felt her presence still and knew she was waiting. I put my face against the warm stone and felt the beating hearts of a thousand, the earth itself a beating heart that had been close to death countless times and would die yet, but not for eons to come, and I still had a ways to go. I left the clearing and walked on, disappearing into the trees and beyond. Within I saw visions and chimeras, priestesses and kouroi, and nymphs who supped wine from Dionysian horns and ate plums from between the bosoms of goddesses. In the realms of vision, gods do not have eyes for men. I passed unnoticed, thirsty as I was and in need of their diaphanous wine.

I came across their temple, ruined as it was even in its days of splendor, for the temples contained within them all times past and present and were at the height of beauty in their eternal form, which is the form of ruin exquisite; I saw in its arrangement the building of it and the tumbling of its columns too. The perfection of it was in the isochronal destiny of its destitution. Creation and demise and all between therein. Amidst its crumbling columns and dazzling marble, and golden capitals and statues faceless with aging, I felt her heartbeat. Then I saw, flickering now in the silver light of the moon, the hem of her dress as she disappeared behind a column, only to reappear some distance away behind the marble statue of a wood nymph. The warm trickle of her laughter was like water from the marble vase of a cherub in a renaissance fountain. That laughter the death of me, extinguishing my soul. I follow it, see the silver flash of silk chimeric in the moonlight, and take chase, laughter and light, light and laughter. *Selena, Selena…*

She takes me to the trees. Takes me out of the light into darkness. But she is light, she is darkness. She is moonlight to my soul.

She dances. She flies. I die nightly in pursuit of her but come alive in the chase. I pause by a clump of spurge which has caught and torn a portion of her dress. I take the tiny square of silk and smell it; it smells of night and rain and stone. She sleeps on a bed of marble and wakes in cold moonless nights, wondering why I have not come for her. This is my terror, what haunts my sleep. She hates me because I have forgotten. I put the silk in my mouth and resume the hunt.

Dragons here, and nymphs and gods. Men do not belong in a place of resurrection. She is close now. I feel her. Her laughter caresses my face like a soft breeze. I catch sight of her shoulder, like the cheek of the moon as it rises over Psiloritis. I almost catch hold of her dress but she escapes me, loses me in a thick copse of datura. Her laughter bades. I extricate myself and run blindly through the trees; should I lose her, I am lost. My soul bereft, there is nothing left but emptiness, and emptiness is worse than death.

Blind, I stumble into the clearing. She is there, I have found her. On the altar, she lies waiting, one thigh emerging from the folds of silk, draped over the edge of the alter. A hand on her breast. I come up next to her. No matter how I try, I cannot focus on her face. But the laugh is unmistakable.

Selena the moonlight, Selena in the light of the moon…

She takes my hand and lays it on her beating breast. I feel her heartbeat quicken. The laughter has ceased. I climb onto her, reach down and tear at the silk. Silver like the moonlight, it tears in my hand. I stuff it into my mouth. She parts her legs. Then she raises her hand, in it a knife, pearl and moonstone the hilt, Damascus the blade.

Vangelis, my good angel, she whispers, and her breath blows through me and pierces my soul. She places the blade into my hand, enclasps my hands in hers. *I shall never be free…*

I plunge the knife into her heart, close my eyes and lay my head on her belly, the silver dress now stained with blood. When I raise my head again, I am sitting atop the great lizard, the knife embedded in its still beating heart.

I want your soul, it whispers…

I opened my eyes and sat up. My face was wet and I was shaking, and my T-shirt moist with sweat. I put my head in my hands and cursed silently. Then I screamed.

4

The roads were dead, only the streets around the edges of the Mercantile with any traffic. The curb-crawlers were out among the nightwalkers: shifty-looking, diminutive Mexican putas alongside six-foot transvestites, and the big fat black whores who attracted a very specific clientele, mostly small white males with middling jobs, for whom conquering a gargantuan prostitute would be the affirmation they needed in life. Pimps and dealers lurking in the shadows. A whole economy conducted after dark, and with the connivance of the law, who took a step back and let the underground commerce take its course. No accident, of course, that the city's red-light district came to be on the edge of the Mercantile, fueled as it was, in large part, by the white-collar trade of the executives who drove many of the cars that now prowled the streets. Bored by wealth and power, they were the ones no longer excited by fine and expensive things, whose only remaining thrills were to be found in the perilous, the vulgar and the seedy. And why not. We all need to get down and dirty sometimes.

I parked the car in a backstreet car park. The place was closed and the attendant gone, but there were two other cars there and it was better than leaving it on the street.

I looked down at the phone which lay on the passenger-side seat. I picked it up and went to turn it off, but thinking better of it I left it be and put it in the glove box instead. Then I got out and locked the car. I proceeded down the street and into the outskirts of Chinatown.

I knocked the door with some hesitancy. It was after two and I didn't know if he'd be open. A place like this, though, he had to be keeping odd hours. A minute or two later, I heard him coming up the stairs. Then the door opened, the hinges giving a metallic shriek.

'Fuck aye, pal. Welcome back to the dream shebeen. What is it brings you here on this dark and lonely night?' he said in greeting. I glanced over my shoulder. 'Maybe you should come on in.'

He turned down the stairs and I stepped inside, shutting the door and following him to the basement.

All the dreamers were here. Only two seats free in his hive, the rest occupied. This the opium den of the modern city, where people came to lose themselves, their faces caught in a plethora of affectations depending on their particular 'poison': some at peace, some in awe, some in gruesome contortion and some in ecstasy. All silent, their journey in the mind's eye only. That journey somehow painted on the face, though, an evocative window into the soul's repose. Here they came to live, and perhaps to die.

'What is it you're looking for tonight, pal?' He sat down in his chair at the operating station.

I looked around at the faces one final time and turned to him. 'You do dream stripping?'

He grimaced, sucking the air in through his teeth. 'Ah, fuck sake – why couldn't you have asked me for something nice and harmless, like Gimp, or Gogo? What you wanna go and get into stripping for? Hah? Fuckin' dangerous, pal. Fuckin' dangerous.'

'I know the risks.' I took a roll of bills from my pocket. 'I'll pay.'

'Fuck sake.' He scratched his stubbled chin. 'And here's me

thinkin' this was gonna be a nice quiet night…'

He turned to the console, sighing, and punched a few buttons. He shook his head. 'See you cunts come in here think you know a thing or two about the meta, and think you can go pokin' around in there without consequences…'

He trailed off, turning back to me. 'Look, pal. I'm gonna gie ye one last chance to say no, alright. Cause it's a lot of work for me, and it's risky as fuck for y—'

I took the SD card from my pocket and held it out. He shut up for long enough to take it from my hand.

'This the dream?'

I nodded.

'And you built it?'

'I did.'

He shook his head. 'Fuck sake. I hope to Christ you know what you're doing. 'Cause I take no responsibility for your work – or your fuck-ups, as the case may be. You get me?'

'Sure,' I said. I took off my jacket. 'Now can we stop chatting and get on with it?'

He shook his head again. 'Right. A grand, pal. Up front, if you please. And I don't do disclaimers. You walk outta here and you're a little fucked in the head, that's your problem.'

I put the money on the table.

'Alright then.' He put the SD in the machine and loaded the card. The raw data came up onscreen. He looked at it for several seconds, then turned to look at me. 'Just what is it you do, pal?' He turned back to the screen. 'You know what – don't answer that. I do not want to fuckin' know. I just hope this is clean…'

He ran a malware check on the card.

'Alright then.' He turned to me. 'Go and take yourself a seat.'

I made for an empty chair.

'You know there's no safety word in dream stripping, don't ya? Once the program's running, that's it. You're in it to win it.'

I nodded. 'I know.'

I sat down in the chair. He got up and went to a drawer, taking out an epidural. He wired it up and applied it to the back of my neck. I sat back in the chair and took a deep breath.

'Aye, get yersel' ready, partner. This may sting a little…'

He sat down at the station and prepped the program and quickly ran the sequence I'd built to check for splicing errors. He caught sight of Selena among the mad array of the dream.

'Christ, would you look at that angel – and this is what you wanna go stripping?' He turned to look at me.

'If I find you've harvested any of that, I'll fucking kill you,' I said.

'Hey, I got enough of my own nightmares, pal. I dinnae need yours too.' He scratched his unshorn cheek then flexed his neck, and sighed deeply. 'Right then. Let's get to work…'

He glanced at me once over his shoulder, in his eyes a warning that there was no turning back. I nodded. He turned back to the console. 'If you're gonna dine with cannibals, darlin', then sooner or later you're gonna get eaten…'

He pushed the button.

A swelling rush tore up my spine, and the bright flash originating at the top of my spinal cord subsumed my whole being. When I opened my eyes, I was back in the boat by the vast shore. My eyes were wet. I wiped them and sat up. The sky above was lit with stars. I climbed out of the boat and onto the shore.

When my feet touched the earth I felt a tremor. I turned to look at the sea, seeing it shudder and vibrate as if it was a glass of water on a table that someone had just knocked against. Then again. Like the footfall of a very large animal, large enough to shake the world. I realized what was happening and why I was there. I turned to look toward the trees.

Selena, I whispered. Then I ran.

I ran fast as I could into the trees as the deep tremors drew closer. I felt those vibrations right to my bones. My head stung with white noise. I tripped and stumbled and pelted through the woods blindly, searching, searching…

Selena! I shouted. *Selena!*

The ground underfoot began to glow with a kind of amethyst resonance and it grew hotter. The throbbing tremors reached a fever pitch. Then I stumbled into the clearing. There she was, on the altar. I rushed toward the center, the booming now threatening to engulf us. She sat up and turned to me, and I came to a standstill, staring at her in disbelief. It wasn't her, it was…

Celeste.

She held up a hand. *Don't be afraid… I've come to take you back. Trust me, you don't want to do this…*

I screamed: *Selena! Selena!*

Just as the tremors came down on top of us, she threw herself upon me—

I opened my eyes and gasped. Back in the hive, disorientated. Head spinning. Nauseous. I turned to look at the guy, then turned my head the other way. Celeste was reclining next to me, plugged into the hive.

I groaned, reaching up to pull the epidural from my neck. 'You motherfucker,' I hissed. I got up off the chair. He stood up.

'Just hold on now, pal – she said it was alright, that it was what you wanted—'

'You let her in my fucking head!' I gripped him by the throat. 'You scumbag, I told you what I wanted – I gave you the program, and you let her fucking ambush me!'

'She said it was what you wanted!'

I raised a fist to strike him, but a hand restrained my arm. When I turned, she was holding me back. I let go of him and turned to her.

'What do you think you're doing?' I said.

'Wait…' She raised a hand. 'It was them, it was Vathos. And I can prove it to you.'

I let her take me out of there to her car. My mind felt jagged, like something was out of place. Otherwise I might've hurt her. She was alone, none of the others with her. But they had to have put her up to it.

'They're using you,' I said, when we'd got into the car.

'How do you know I'm not using them?'

'You think you're in control, do you? You don't know what you're messing with, truly. One or all of you are gonna end up dead. Trust me.'

'My son's dead. I don't care if I die too. The only hurt that'll cause me is if I don't see the men who killed my son die before I do.'

I sighed and shook my head. 'You people are dreamers. You think you have a cause, but you don't see how the world truly is. This is not going to go away, no matter how you fight it. Vathos is only a small part of the machine.'

'Why don't you save judgment until I show you what I have to show you…'

She reached behind the seat and lifted a folder. I glanced furtively out the window of the car. I still had no idea who these people were. And they weren't even the ones I had to worry about.

She opened the folder. 'You recognize her?' She lifted out a grainy photo and held it up. It was barely visible in the low light of the car. But unease took hold in my stomach all the same. I turned away.

'That could be anybody,' I said.

She shook her head. 'That's her. That's your sister.'

'What do you know about my sister?' I said. 'And who are you anyway? Some woman whose son got himself killed? Well I'm sorry, lady, but you don't know a fucking thing.' I reached for the handle. 'And I swear, if I ever see any of y—'

'This one. Just look at this one.'

I stared at it, chewing the inside of my lip. Then I took it from her. This time there was no doubt. Her face wasn't visible, but it was her, no question. The slope of the shoulder and the tilt of the head. And the overcoat. She looked haunting. Or haunted.

'Where did you get these?' I scrutinized Celeste's face, seeing no sign of ill-intent.

'Eric's team put them together. They've been collecting evidence against Vathos for a long time. You came onto their radar a year or two ago, and they've been searching for a way to reach out to you. This is what they came up with.'

'Where was this taken?'

'Athens.'

'Athens, Greece? What was she doing in Athens?'

She shook her head. 'They don't know all the details. Everything they do know is in here.' She put the folder into my lap. 'They told me to show it to you. But you can't take it home with you. If you want to study the files, you have to do it with their say-so.'

I glanced at her. 'I could just take it.'

She nodded. 'Yes you could. But you know you'd be putting yourself in danger as much as the rest of us.'

I flicked through the file. There were flight records, stills of video footage, emails between Selena and her office. Then what looked like a police report on her disappearance. I raised it to better see.

'What language is that?' I said.

'Serbian. She disappeared in Pristina.'

'Serbian?'

'That police report was later scrubbed. I don't know how they found it, but apparently it wasn't easy to come by.'

I shook my head. My mind was reeling. Not only from the procedure I'd nearly gone through in the dream shop, but now this.

'So what has all this to do with Vathos?' I said.

She reached into the folder and pulled out a series of papers at the back, and opened them out for me to see.

'Because at the same time your sister disappeared, there were agents from your company in Pristina. Look…'

She indicated the passenger list of a flight from Chicago to Belgrade. One name was highlighted:

Viktor Rodin.

5

'How does that gel with the GPR data?'

'Looks good. I think this leads right onto the garden, though. See? There's no foyer.'

I stared at the wall behind Sura and DP in Analeptics, where the picture of a woman under surveillance held my attention. She was in the kitchen, looking out her window into the garden. The picture was taken by drone. I found myself wondering what she was thinking at that very moment; the look on her face was indecipherable. Her eyes were wide with alarm, yet she was almost smiling. For some reason, it struck me that she had to be a prisoner…

'Yeah, that's better.'

'Mm-hmm. Got it.'

'What do you think, Vangelis?'

Locked up, yet did she intuit her impending release?

'Vangelis?'

'Huh?' I turned to see DP and Sura staring at me.

'Did you hear what I said?'

'What'd you say, DP?'

He shook his head. 'Fuckin' daydreamer. Get with it, man. Sura has just okayed the draft blueprint. You wanna have a look at it, or you wanna go back to La-La Land where you were oh-so happily dreaming?'

'Screw yourself, dipshit. Just show me the blueprint.'

'Here.' He turned the laptop to me and hit play, and a mock-up of the dream locale played. I nodded along absentmindedly.

'Yeah, yeah… looks great. Where's that labyrinth we talked about, though? I don't see it.'

'Fuckwit, I just said a minute ago we were gonna put it in later.'

I nodded. 'Yeah, I got ya.'

He shook his head. 'Space cadet.' Then he stood up and closed his laptop. 'Right, I'm gonna go lock myself away and put on some earphones and finish this. Anybody need anything, don't come knocking.'

He looked at me once before going out the door. I stood up to go. Sura closed her folder and rose from the table.

'Hey, you okay?'

'What? Yeah, I'm fine.'

'You seem a little out of sorts. Like your head's somewhere else or something.'

I took a deep breath and sighed. 'Just… nah, it's nothing. Life. Bullshit.'

She lowered her voice. 'Yeah well, maybe you keep an eye on it, especially around here. That kind of thing doesn't go unnoticed. Know what I mean?'

'Yeah, I know what you mean.'

She stepped out into the corridor and I followed her out.

'I'm done now, might stop and have a beer on the way home. Wanna join me?'

'Didn't take you for a drinker,' I said.

'Used to be, not anymore. Sometimes I have one just to remind myself what I'm not missing. Wanna take a trip down memory lane with me?'

'Not my memories, but sure, I'll come along. I was just leaving anyway. I'll follow you in the car.'

Sura drove over to Perry Street, right on the edge of the Sprawl. She parked up in a side-street car park and I parked beside her. When she'd given her keys to the attendant, a guy she seemed to know, we went out into the street.

'Fuck are we doing here?' I said to her as we turned down Perry Street. She grinned.

'Don't tell me you're spooked, Agent Zervas?' she said, grinning.

'Cut it with the "Agent" shit, will you?'

'Relax. I'm not gonna out you to the locals. We wouldn't walk out of here.'

I looked up and down the street. It wasn't quite the skid row that the Sprawl was, but it was where things started to go downhill. Not a place you'd be found hanging out if you had concerns about your reputation.

'So, this your old stomping ground?'

She nodded. 'Of course, ten years ago it wasn't like this. Ten years ago it was all bohemian and hipster. Now it's gone all to shit. But there's a corner or two that still retain the old charm.'

'Bull*shit*. This place is skanky as it gets. Even the prostitutes have moved out.' I turned to see a girl in a doorway with a crack pipe, trying desperately to get flame from her lighter. 'Apart from her...'

'Don't be gettin' down on the working girls. A place like this, it must be brutal on them.'

I didn't reply. Sura turned down an alley off Perry Street, and I was surprised to see a wire fence with a gate in it, and beyond, a 'beer garden', if you could call it that: A bunch of picnic tables and some colored lighting strung across the alley. Music played from speakers above a door that led into the back of the bar.

'What do you think?' Sura said, opening the gate into the garden.

I shook my head. 'I never cease to wonder. And it doesn't even smell of shit.'

'Prick.'

We got a couple of beers and sat down at a table in the garden.

'Cheers.' She held up her bottle.

'Cheers.'

We had a drink then sat in silence for a bit. I looked around the garden, this little slice of bohemian, beatnik heaven. Palm fronds dangling from wires strung over our heads. Gaudy plastic flamingoes in one corner, and the walls covered with retro aluminum advertising signs. Ten years ago I might've even appreciated a joint like this myself.

'Flamingoes,' I said.

'Uh-huh. What about 'em?'

'Unforgivable.'

Sura smiled. 'What if I told you I stole one one night when I was drunk and I still have it in my apartment?'

'Nah, you didn't…'

She nodded and smiled, then shook her head. 'I love that fucking flamingo, and I don't know why…'

'It's sentimental. Symbolic. Of a life you once had and will never have again.'

'Maybe.' She smiled, looking away over my head somewhere. 'Yeah, I dunno how I got where I am now. I was *not* the corporate type. At all.'

'You still aren't. You're an operative.'

She glanced around her, then shook her head. 'Still a corporate hack. I know what we do, who we work for.'

'And you got no qualms about it?'

'Do you?' She stared at me intently, her eyes roving over my face. She'd been through the same basic training as I had. I knew what she was looking for.

'We do what we do because it speaks to some deep part of us, an itch that needs scratching, or maybe retribution for our own personal ills. Hell, fucked if I really know why I do it, but I do. And a part of me even likes it.' I sipped the beer and put the bottle down. 'Most days.'

She nodded. 'Yeah. But what you do and I do are very different.'

'Like you say, we know who we work for.'

'Yeah.' She took a drink, then put the bottle down and turned it slowly on the table. 'You know, I had a dream last night where I took my mother by the throat and punched her till her head split open—'

'Jesus fucking Christ... why you telling me this?'

'Is it because of what we do? Are we fucked up for life? Are we scarring ourselves by our jobs?'

I shook my head. 'I don't know, Sura. Jesus, I've no idea what shit you went through as a kid. Maybe you had a fucked-up relationship with your mother, I dunno. I do *not* have the answers to questions like that...'

'You ever think about things like that?'

'Sure I do.' I turned away and sighed. 'Sure I do.'

'You dream fucked-up stuff?'

'Yeah. I try not to sleep too much.'

She jabbed a finger in my direction. 'Now *that's* messed up.' She turned to look around the beer garden. 'You know what else is messed up? I wish I still smoked.'

'Never did get a taste for it. Fucking disgusting habit if you ask me,' I said.

'Yeah, it's a strange one. Like, why do the things that kill us fastest feel the best?'

'I lived, I wined, I died, and in all the stifling beauty of the soul's demise,' I said.

Sura frowned. 'What's that?'

I shrugged, surprised even myself. 'Dunno. Must have read it somewhere.' I thought of Roche for some reason.

'Never took you for a poet.'

'I've never read a line of poetry in my life,' I said.

'Hmm.' Sura picked up her beer, watching me carefully over the bottle as she drank. I looked away, pretending I wasn't aware of her gaze.

'What's the worst thing you ever did?' she asked then.

'In work?'

She shrugged.

'You know I can't answer that…'

'I know.' She clasped her hands together as if in prayer. 'Outside work, then.'

I shook my head and sighed. 'My whole life has been one long series of sins and omissions, Sura.'

She smiled wryly. 'There's more information contained in what you don't say, Zervas, than what you do. Anyone ever tell you that?'

'Not in so many words.'

'One of those things, huh?'

'What things?'

'Things you know about yourself but can't put into words until someone else does it for you.'

'This your usual beer talk?' I said.

'There you go again – evasion.'

'Must be my modus operandi.'

Sura tilted her bottle at me. 'The thirst for deception is greater than that for knowledge.'

'So who the fuck said that, then?'

Sura winked. 'Pick up a book sometime, dipshit.'

With Roche on my mind, I made an appointment and drove over to her place. It had been a few weeks since she'd worked on me, and the itch to continue with the backpiece and some other indefinable urge to see her compelled me. At nine-thirty, I knocked on her door. She answered in her usual way, laconically and with an air of mild irritation, as if dealing with people was the price she had to pay to practice her art.

'If you came to fuck, forget it. I'm on my period.'

'I came by to get work done, Roche.'

'Want me to stick a finger in your asshole? You that kinda guy?'

'What? No… fuck sake. I came for the tattoo.' I took off my jacket.

'I was joking.'

'You can't tell jokes, Roche. Don't try.'

'I'm post-irony. You just don't get me.'

'No I do not, Roche. No I do not.'

'Lie down.'

I took off my shirt and lay down on the table. She had the needles already prepped. I felt her hand run up my spine and I felt goosebumps on the back of my neck. She must have noticed.

'Sure you don't want me to finger you?'

'Fuck off.'

When she spoke again, I heard a smile in her words. I'd never seen her smile.

'You know some turtles breathe through their assholes?'

I sighed. 'I did not know that, Roche.'

'Would you like to hear more, or will I tell you about fucking my ex with a strap-on?'

'Maybe we just forget about asses and assholes, Roche, how about that?'

'Hmm…'

She paused, two fingers stretching the flesh of my back.

'What is it?' I said.

'There's something here I didn't tattoo on you…'

'What? You mean *ink*?'

'Yes. Are you seeing someone else?'

'Don't talk crazy, Roche – it's just you.'

'Then what is this…?' She turned to the counter and lifted a small magnifying glass, holding it close to my upper right shoulder.

'Well, what the fuck is it?' I said.

She was quiet as she examined my back. 'A glyph. Something. Maybe nothing. A circle, with a line through it… maybe *theta*.'

'Theta? What the fuck is "theta"?'

'Aren't you Greek? You don't know theta?' I tried to sit up but she held me down. 'Don't move.'

'I'm not "Greek Greek", if you know what I mean. You sure you didn't do it? Maybe you were stoned and forgot about it.'

'I know what I did and didn't do.' I heard the irritation in her voice. 'If I find out you've been letting someone else work on my tattoo, you'll be getting more than a finger in your ass, I can promise you.'

'Jesus Christ, Roche, I wouldn't let anyone fuck with your work.'

She sighed. 'This is strange.'

'You gonna tattoo over it?'

'I can't, without fucking up the image. I'll leave it for now. Just don't come back to me with any more surprises, okay?'

'I don't know how the fuck it got there, Roche.'

'Shut up and be still.'

The gun buzzed.

After we were done, we sat and smoked a joint. My back throbbed with the pain of the fresh trauma, something the dope only served to accentuate. I looked up at Sura's bookshelf.

'Hey, you know about poetry and stuff, right?' I said.

She shrugged. 'I read a little.'

'If I tell you something can you tell me where it's from?'

'I dunno. Try me.' She puffed idly on the joint as she looked at the ceiling. I told her the thing I'd said to Sura at the bar. Roche shook her head. 'Never heard it before.' She passed me the joint. 'Google it.'

I shook my head then took a puff. 'Don't need to know that badly.'

'But you do want to know about theta,' she said.

'What I want to know,' I said, 'is how something got on my back that you didn't tattoo there.' I looked at her. Her eyes narrowed.

'Maybe you are cursed,' she said.

'Fuck are you talking about?' I handed the joint back to her. 'Don't be filling my head with that shit.'

'Stigmata…'

'Drop it, Roche. I don't wanna hear any voodoo shit.'

She watched me as I smoked at the joint. Finally, she sighed and turned away. 'The ancient Egyptians had a symbol like theta. The circle represented the cosmos, and the line through the middle a snake encircling the world.'

'Am I the snake, Roche, is that what you're saying?'

She stood up. 'Maybe you are, and maybe you are not. And maybe the snake is bad, and maybe the snake is good. Either way, it doesn't matter. I am hungry, and it's time for you to go.'

6

Driving home from work in the evening a day later, I felt a surge of anger when I saw the sign. I was nearing the exit for my apartment when it flashed up on the highway message board:

SISTEMA CENTRAL EN FUNCTIONAMENTO

I bit my lip and shook my head, determined to drive on. But when I swerved at the last minute to come off at the exit, I grew furious at myself.

'Fuck!'

I smacked the wheel of the car. Coming off the slip road onto the suburban road, I looked around frantically for another sign of their presence. It came: the roadside sign of the gas station I was passing at that moment flickered momentarily to display an unmistakable prompt:

SMA

I pulled in at the gas station, parking at the back and killing the engine. I took my phone from the inside pocket of my jacket and flicked it on, before chucking it in the glovebox.

'Sons of bitches,' I said. I got out of the car.

I locked the car and looked around, seeing no one. I went in the door of the gas station. Inside there was only the attendant. I watched him for a moment to see if he was one of them, but he gave no sign. I grabbed a bottle of soda from the fridge and paid for it, simply so I didn't look out of place. Then I went back outside.

'Maybe I'm going fucking crazy,' I muttered, taking a sip from the bottle. I stood there in the forecourt, looking around, seeing nothing. I went back to the car.

I was just about to get back in and drive away, when I saw a light flashing in the window of an unfinished apartment block on a building site out back of the gas station. It flickered again.

It had to be them. Still angry, I walked toward the fence that surrounded the building site and pushed through, and made my way across the dark uneven expanse of the site. Piles of reinforced steel and breeze blocks were scattered here and there. Portajohns dotted the grounds. I glanced up at the window to see the light. Second floor.

The door to the building, when I reached it, was open. I tossed the bottle of soda away and went in.

Inside it was quiet. I was waiting for one of them to come out of the shadows, but no one appeared.

'Where are you?' I spoke to the dark. There was no answer.

The fire exit lights identified the stairs, and I went through the door and ascended. Two floors and into the hallway. The smell of cement and fresh paint. Bare wood. About halfway down, a door was open. I glanced inside.

Celeste was standing to the side of the window with the lit lamp, the man in the overcoat sitting at a small table. A man I hadn't seen before was leaning against the wall to my left. I went in and stopped in the middle of the floor. The three of them watched me silently.

'How about you leave off with your Pavlovian fuckery, huh?' I said. 'I feel like you're inside my head.'

The guy at the table spoke. 'You get in other people's head for a living, Vangelis. What makes you think you're exempt? Or maybe that's why you're upset, because you thought you were.'

'Maybe next time you just push a note under my front

door, what do you say?'

'You know we can't do that.'

I shook my head. 'No, you can't. But I don't appreciate being treated like some hopping dog.'

'Don't like it when it's you getting the runaround, huh?' the guy by the wall said. I glared at him. The man at the table silenced his partner with a glance.

'We need an answer, Vangelis. Are you in or are you out?' I looked at the woman. She fixed me in a restive gaze. 'We need to move on what we have. We can't keep hanging on for you. We need an answer.'

I looked around the room before settling my eyes on him. 'What would it entail? From my side?'

He sighed and nodded. 'We'd need you to get us access to the Vathos servers. That's it.'

I shook my head. 'I put so much as a USB stick in a stack at work, it triggers security. Forget it. The hardware is unassailable.'

'There's another way…'

'Oh yeah? How's that?'

'We're working on it. We haven't done the final testing yet, but we feel very good about it. Give us a few more days.'

'You're feelin' "very good". Jesus fucking Christ, you people must be nuts.'

The guy reached into the pocket of his overcoat and took out a pack of cigarettes, extracting one and lighting it.

'We know what we're asking, and we know it's a big ask, one that requires a good deal of trust on your part. But believe me when I say it's the only way to do this and succeed. We don't have the resources to go up against Vathos's firewalls – they're too powerful. But this…' He leaned forward, resting his arms on the table. '…this is the chink in their armor. They won't see it coming at all.'

'You know there are firewalls around all our programs too, don't you? Weapons prohibitions, coding alarms, intrusion fail-safes, right? I mean, you can't just step out of the program right into the mainframe system. It's not that fucking easy.'

'We believe we have a back door. We've tested it on a Vathos program we retrieved and it didn't trigger any alarms.'

'But you haven't tested it in a live environment?'

'Of course not. We can't, obviously.'

I glanced from one to the other again. 'So what? Just gonna try it out and me as the guinea pig, huh? Real nice of you.'

The man took an aggravated puff of his cigarette. 'The probability of success is high.'

'Ah.' I laughed and shook my head. 'The probability. Uh-huh. Well, let me tell you something about probability. I have numbers thrown at me every day – 98 percent, 86 percent, the numbers are the numbers, the figures are good… well, you know what I've learned about the numbers?' I raised my head questioningly. 'The numbers don't mean shit. Shit goes wrong, no matter what. You can throw all the numbers at me you like, but the fact remains – something is going to go sideways.'

'Everything has a risk,' the guy at the wall said.

'Just in this case, it's all me. You'll be tucked away in some little basement somewhere, it'll be me that gets dragged into a room and subjected to fuck-knows-what, and maybe end up in a ditch with a bullet in the back of the head.'

The guy at the table nodded slowly. 'It seems you understand the people you work for better than we thought.'

'I know who I work for, alright.'

'So you believe they're the ones who made your sister disappear,' Celeste said, speaking up for the first time. She stepped toward me. 'Well, this is the only way you're going to find out the truth.'

I stared at her for a second then turned back to the man at the table. 'So what, you're gonna waltz on out of my head into the mainframe, go digging around and find out some shit about Selena, is that it?' I laughed out loud.

'You know it's the only way,' she said.

'Dreamers, all of you.'

The man nodded. 'Yes, we are. But dreamers who're determined, and know how to get the job done. If we say we'll do it, we'll do it.'

We all fell silent. I sighed and walked toward the window, and looked outside. Same old city, same old starless skies. Looking out at the punk smudge of the city in front of me, I was filled with a sudden feeling of rottenness. It was the city, it was me. And it was all filthy.

I turned to the three hopeless rebels and nodded. 'Okay. I'll do it. I wanna sit down with your tech guy though. I'm not jumping into this unless I'm convinced he knows exactly what he's doing.'

He nodded. 'We can do that.'

'Alright then.'

I looked at Celeste. The glimmer in her eye told me how much she wanted this. It still wasn't enough to blot out the instinctive revulsion she held for me. It remained. She couldn't hide that.

'I'm Eric,' the guy at the table said. He gestured over his shoulder. 'That's Marko.'

'Yeah? You band of misfits have a name? Some vainglorious handle?'

Eric shook his head. 'We're just concerned citizens, a handful of disparate souls who want justice.'

I shook my head. 'Justice…' I spat out the word. 'Justice is a pipe dream.'

'Ain't that always been the way,' he said ruefully. Then he smiled. 'But it ain't for love of tryin'.'

I got in the chair while DP loaded the base program.

'You miss me?' he said, punching buttons on the keyboard.

'Did I fuck,' I said, settling in.

'Aww, and I thought you'd be lost without me.'

'DP,' I said, 'the day I miss you is the day I put the cold barrel of a gun in my mouth and kiss it all goodbye.'

He grinned. 'I know you love me really.'

'Just load the program, dipshit.'

He hit the button. 'Putting you in, partner. Say hello to your old friend the Structure…'

Blinding light and a searing flash, and I was thrust into the metaconscious framework, deep in the chasms of residual consciousness.

—No hanging about, partner. Loading you straight into the program.

There was a shudder in the vast emptiness around me and I was suddenly surrounded by green: grass underfoot, trees up ahead, an enormous hedge behind me. Above me, the sky dark and clouded. I heard a wolf.

'Why's there a wolf howlin', DP?'

—Got a little surprise for you partner. We're gonna run a little trainin' exercise.

'Oh yeah? Gonna give me a crossbow and send me out hunting?'

—Nah, my man. You're not doing the hunting. It's you being hunted.

'Are you kidding me?' There was a sudden knot in my gut.

—Sorry, partner. Analytics signed off on it yesterday, told me not to tell you. It's designed to improve your 'instinctual readiness' and 'empathic situational awareness', ya get me? Fucking Analytics with their big words.

I looked around. I was in the mock-up landscape for the upcoming operation, presumably on the target's estate. I had a rough awareness of the territory. I kicked myself for not paying closer attention to the program development when we were prepping for DP's build.

'Here's an idea – why don't you pop yourself into the program, DP, and I'll introduce you to some hunting?'

—You can gut me later. Right now you need to get moving pal. The pack is on the move. And they're moving right in your direction…

'Motherfucker,' I said. I scanned the immediate area and moved off, heading south. 'Well, are you gonna give me something to defend myself with, asshole?'

—Shit, almost forgot – here…

A blade materialized on my hip.

'A knife. Great. I need to get up close and personal, do I? Cheers.'

—Analytics, bud. What can I do.

'You can go and fuck yourself, is what you can do.'

—Signin' off now partner. You're on your own. I'll only be back when either you or the wolves are dead.

'Yeah, go on and piss off then.'

—Enjoy.

The line went dead and I was on my own in the dark, moving over a baleful terrain. I tried to map the land out in my head, drawing on vague memories of the program build. Another howl erupted in the vast silence of the night, snapping me back to the present moment.

'Fucking wolves,' I muttered. How could I go up against a pack of wolves anyway? How many were even in a pack? Five, six? Seven? I'd have to try and pick them off one by one. But how…

I picked up speed, leaping over a gate into a small field. On the other side of the field I was sure were the gardens of the target's estate. I ran straight across, glancing east. There was a full moon. Some prick down in Analytics must have thought they were very clever – wolves and a full moon. What a cliché. Didn't make it any less tangible though.

I crossed the field and leapt over a small stile to the other side. Now I could see the mansion. Off behind it, the barns. I did a quick calculation: gardens or the barn? Barn seemed like the better option – if all else failed I could hide in the rafters. Maybe there'd be something I could arm myself with. In a split second, I was moving toward the barns.

I reconnoitered the house as I moved. A single light on in the upper floors. A study, if I remembered correctly. The target lived alone with only a skeleton staff, none of whom stayed overnight. I had a sudden jarring sensation, like why was he at home? Didn't matter. The program would run without his input. His presence in the house was merely symbolic.

I crossed the expanse between the field and the barn, reaching the doors as I heard another howl. I stopped and turned, and scanned everything between myself and the wooded area off to the west. I saw nothing. My heart pounding now, I opened the doors and slipped inside.

Inside it was impossibly dark but my eyes soon adjusted. I scanned the place. In the center of the floor was a tractor. Running down the sides of it, two workbenches. I quickly walked down one side, scanning the benches for anything of use. My eyes alighted on a hand scythe and I picked it up. Couldn't hurt having two blades. Nothing else of use, merely an assortment of tools and other paraphernalia. I came down the other side, finding nothing else. I heard a howl from beyond the barn and my senses snapped alert. Closer now. How were they hunting? I jumped onto the ladder and shimmied up into the loft. I crept over to the large transom window to peer out into the night. Certainly they weren't hunting by smell – this was a program. Maybe they were hunting to some AI rendering of smell, based on my heart rate and body temperature, and how much I'd be sweating if it were a real-life scenario. Or maybe those pricks in Analytics had simply rigged the game. I wiped the window to better see outside. Still could see nothing. But I could feel them, as if they were some deep intrinsic part of me. The ghost in my machine. I strained my eyes, looking out over the yard to the fields beyond, behind the trees. Then I saw movement, a dark shadow coming over the hillock: the pack, four of them. No – five. I swore silently. My chest tightened. I focused on my breathing as I watched them come down toward the house and the barns, the haunting moonlight casting a glow over the pack all the way to the yard outside. And as they drew near, I saw their eyes: a deep crystalline blue, unlike any wolf I'd ever seen. But then this was the fantasy of some grunt in Analytics; to be fair, the purpose of the task was to make it as disturbing as possible. This knowledge brought me little reassurance, though. I watched the pack, one after the other, slip through the gate in the fence that led into the grounds of the house. They were silent now, and their trot had slowed to an amble, as they nosed the ground following whatever scent it was that would lead them to their quarry. Me. I watched their lithe bodies as they padded forward, their eyes glinting silver when they lifted their noses from the ground. Eyes that saw much, more than I did. I hunkered there absolutely still, watching as one separated from the pack and trotted toward the barn. I lowered myself and put my face to the wood floor. Through the slats of the floor I could see into the barn below. I lay absolutely still. Unmoving. First I heard the panting, then saw the hot breath. Then the head came through the door, ears alert, head shifting side to side. My palms felt damp against the cool wood. I felt my chest thud against the floor. The wolf paused directly below me. Sniffed the air. My body was tense but I breathed lightly and silently. The watcher. The animal raised its head a touch and I froze, seeing the tongue lolling in its jaws. Then he patted the ground with his forepaw, turned, and trotted out of the barn. I let out a soft sigh, and pushed my hands against the floor to peel myself up. Before I rose to my feet, through the slats I saw a pitchfork in the corner against the door, which I hadn't seen on my way in. I got up on my knees and peered out the window, seeing the animal pad in the direction of the house. I could see three other animals close by the back door of the mansion. One I couldn't see. I decided to make for the gardens. Had I been quick enough, I could've picked off the single wolf in the barn, but it was a missed opportunity. I'd be ready next time I had one of them alone.

Silently, carefully, I got up and made my way to the ladder and climbed down. I went straight to the corner and lifted the pitchfork. Then I crept to the door and peered outside. The pack had disappeared behind the house. I scanned the yard for the last one, listening carefully. Still no sign of it. Between myself and the gardens it seemed to be clear.

'If I die I'm takin' at least one of 'em with me,' I whispered, testing the pitchfork in my hands. Then I darted from the barn on my hunkers.

I glanced up as I crossed the yard – still that one light on above in the house. Perhaps I wasn't the only watcher on this night. I made my way past the bay window on the left side of the house, heading directly for the steps that led down into the gardens. Once next to the hedge, I paused, casting a glance behind me to see if the wolves had emerged from the other side of the house. They hadn't. I turned and slipped down the steps into the parterre below. Avoiding the gravel pathways, I stole onto the lawn and made my way, half running, toward the fountain in the center. Beyond the French gardens were the woodlands which would afford me the most cover. Staying low, I followed the hedges taking as much cover as I could. From the house behind me I heard another howl. My chest tightened. The nearness of it meant I felt it as a physical thing, a visceral response. The more I heard it, the more I felt the beast within coil in readiness.

At the far end of the garden I saw a movement and froze, coming to a standstill and crouching low as I could go. My eyes wide in the dark, I watched. Waited. Then I saw it…

A lone wolf, nose to the ground. On the scent. My hand gripped the shaft of the pitchfork tighter and I glanced down at my waist to check for the blade. I breathed in through my nose, not taking my eyes from the beast. But a watched beast knows it is watched. It felt my eyes, the head turning in my direction. Body to the ground, I crept backward until I was at the hedge again. I slipped in behind the hedgerow end, taking one last look at the beast still scanning the gardens, looking for his prey. I slipped around the other side and made my way in the direction of the woodland. It would take me closer to the animal, but with any luck I could slip past and into the trees.

Over the grass silently I moved. Pitchfork at my side, ready.

Man against beast. I felt a thrill I seldom felt, even in the most extreme jobs I'd done. My heart louder than the world around me, I neared the end of the hedge. I paused and took a deep breath. I made a quick calculation: about thirty meters from the end of the garden to the trees beyond. If push came to shove I could be into the treeline and up one of the large oaks on the edge of the woods. Then what? Hide in the trees until DP pulled me out of the program? Fuck. I was getting ready to put my head around the hedge when I heard the growl behind me. I felt it too, inside me. My head bristled, as if a cold electricity crackled over me. I turned my head slowly, feeling the presence of the animal, still not seeing it.

'Are you quick enough?' I whispered, one hand touching the earth, the other gripping the pitchfork.

Again the growl. I glanced over my shoulder in time to see it bound, and I threw myself forward and away from it, turning at the same time to raise the pitchfork. The only thing I saw as it lunged at me were those deadly-blue eyes with a fearless ferocity. The beast came down upon me. The pitchfork slipped into its breast between its two front legs. Impaling itself, it fell with its entire weight on top of me. A terrible animal howl came from its lungs as I was showered with blood. I rolled to the right, tossing the dead weight of the animal from me.

Wasting no time, I leapt to my feet. I looked down at the beast and the contortions of its body, and without a second thought I unsheathed my knife and drove it through its throat. Heart pounding now, I stood up. I heard the pack in the distance, howling now, aware of the death of one of its own. They were coming straight for me. I turned and pelted toward the woods.

A plan? *No plan*. There are no plans when it's life or death. You survive or die. Live on instinct.

The woods, dark and implacable, closed around me. A deep purple hue seeped in at the edges, soon the very fabric of the trees around me seemed to change form: the bark on the trunks was shifting, waving, as if I'd ingested some kind of hallucinogenic. The ground underfoot swimming, throwing me off balance. The boughs of the trees whispering a gentle, threatening hum. And then…

The gentle purple hue took on a silver tinge, and the trunks of the trees began to flatten and sheen until I could see my reflection in them. In all directions, it was me – I was in a wooded hall of mirrors, some of my reflections minuscule, some grotesque, some enormous. All of them poised, ready to leap. I looked down at myself, realizing I was in a crouch with the knife in hand.

'What is this?' I whispered.

I heard the wolves again, just beyond the treeline by the sounds of it. I hurried toward the nearest tree but only saw a reflection of myself which grew in size; there was no tree behind which to hide. I backed away, watching my image recede. When I turned to run in the opposite direction, another gargantuan, repulsive reflection bore down upon me. I picked up a rock and hurled it at the mirror, but the shivering sheen of the mirror merely wobbled, absorbing the rock. I screamed at the mirror, brandishing the blade.

'Come on then, motherfucker, come on…'

I turned. In the mirror behind me saw the first of the wolves. To my right, another. I laughed a crazed laugh and shook my head, getting down on my hunkers, one foot pressed into the earth ready to lunge. The knife clasped in my hand in an ice-pick grip, pressed against my thigh. I raised my eyes to the wolf, the eyes crystalline in their singularity of purpose. It pawed the earth. It keened lowly. I felt it inside me, heard its cravings in my soul, felt its limbs bristle, felt its jaw stretch. One hand on the earth, one on the knife, I saw it brace. There was no space between it and I.

I lunged.

I opened my eyes and sat up in the chair. Gottfried was looking at me, a smirk on his lips. Behind him, Maynes, expressionless but for his cold gaze.

I pulled off the epidural and flexed my neck. 'Christ. So what was that little circus about?'

Maynes sucked air in through his teeth. 'You know we don't question Analytics, Zervas. The job is the reason. We do what we gotta do, no questions.'

'No questions. Uh-huh.' I turned to throw a look at DP. He simply raised his eyebrows as if to absolve himself of all responsibility. 'Nice, guys. Thank you all very much.' I slipped off the chair and reached for my jacket.

'A word please, Agent Zervas, before you go,' said Maynes.

'Sure.' I turned to DP. 'See you later. Prick.'

'Stay safe partner.' He grinned.

I followed Maynes out. He led me silently down the hall to an operations room. I stepped in. Emerson was sitting at the table, perusing a file. Maynes closed the door behind me.

I couldn't keep my mouth shut. 'Not often we see you down here in the mosh pit, sir. To what do we owe the pleasure?'

Emerson looked up, raising an eyebrow. 'You being funny, Zervas?'

'No sir.' I suppressed a grin.

'Then sit down.'

I sat, Maynes taking a seat at the head of the table to my right. I could feel Maynes glaring at me.

Emerson closed the folder and clasped his hands together. 'How'd your little sojourn in the woods go?'

I shook my head. 'Not sure, sir. You'd have to ask Analytics.'

'I already did. It went as well as could be expected.'

'Another reappraisal was it, sir?'

Emerson dismissed my question with a wave of the hand. 'What it was or wasn't is of little importance. All I'll say is, it was of relevance to the operation. What matters now is that we get our heads down and concentrate on what's ahead. Intrusion will begin in three days. Now that you and Analeptics have forged out the base skeleton for the intrusion program, you'll no longer be working together, save for basic operational collaboration. Back to the way things normally work. Are you confident you've fully prepared for the task at hand?'

'Yes sir. I mean, I'm still in the dark about that little episo—'

'I told you, forget it. All you need to worry about is the operation. One hundred percent focus, Zervas, do you hear me?'

'Yes sir.'

He turned to Maynes. 'Everything ready to go?'

Maynes nodded. 'Yes sir. Subversion has all their ducks lined up. Nothing has been overlooked.'

'Good.' He turned back to me. 'It should go without saying, Zervas, that there's a chain of command here at Vathos. As far as you're concerned, I'm at the top of that chain. Below me, and above you, is Maynes here. You understand that, don't you?'

I nodded. 'Sir.'

'So, after your little spat last time, I wanna make sure there aren't gonna be any hiccups like before, you get me? Maynes has been instructed to take a hands-off approach on this one, but if for whatever reason the operation calls for intervention, you need to obey the chain of command, Zervas. Understand?'

'I do sir. Loud and clear.'

He sighed and sat back in the chair. Then he turned to Maynes. He nodded toward the door. Maynes stood, glared at me, and went out, closing the door behind him. Emerson gave me a good once-over.

'You happy, Zervas, doing what you do?'

I nodded. 'Of course sir. I love my job.'

'And you're a good agent. Your aversion to authority aside, you're one of the best we've had through these doors. It would be a shame to let all that talent go to waste.'

I said nothing.

'What I'm getting at, and what you're probably aware of, is that we're keeping an eye on you, Zervas. Toe the line. No more wayward behavior, you hear?'

I nodded. 'Sir.'

'Good. Now get outta here.'

Somehow, I was well down a road there was no going back on. I felt it. I knew it in my bones, but I was compelled to drive on, the demon on one shoulder hissing one thing in my ear, the demon on the other whispering something else. What do you do? You do what you're gonna do, that's what, and it was never any different. Free will? After four years wading through the dregs of my own and other people's subconscious, I no longer believed in it. *Free will…* you are who you are, and nothing is ever gonna change that. Forget the subconscious, forget the mind – it's in your DNA, that's where it is. Your actions, your purpose, your intent – it's biological, in-built. We're all animal. And this mind, these thoughts, are nothing but an evolutionary aberration, a terrible farcical mistake of our development. Fuck it, maybe God did it. Who knows. All I know is, the less you think, the easier life is. And I was thinking way too much about things. Which is how you get into trouble.

'Thank you for coming,' Eric said.

I stepped into the back of the truck and he closed the sliding door behind me.

'Portable console,' I said, looking at the build and the guy sitting at the controls. 'Neat.'

Eric folded his arms and nodded, eyes to the floor. Then he looked up at me. 'This isn't how we normally work, but given our relationship, we can't risk taking you into the heart of our operation. You know how it is.'

'I do, yeah.'

He gestured to the guy sitting at the console. 'This is Verne. Our tech guy.' I nodded a greeting. 'You wanted to see things from our side, Verne is going to run you through it.'

'Alright then,' I said. 'Let me see what you got.'

'Take a seat,' Eric said. I sat down on a stool next to their operator. Verne turned to the console and punched a few buttons.

'So, I believe you're an operative and not a tech guy, is that correct?' he said.

'Yeah, but I know enough. Enough to know if you're bullshitting me or not.'

The guy nodded. 'Nobody's here to bullshit anyone. I'm the best at what I do, so I don't need to. If you'll let me show you...'

He turned to the console and started punching keys. I watched as he brought up some raw program data, and saw its virtual imprint on the other screen.

'This is a Vathos program we got our hands on from – well, that's not important...' He glanced over his shoulder at Eric. '...but by reverse engineering the source code we were able to engineer an insertion point into the Vathos mainframe. Because the source code is built to run on System A, we—'

'Built to run on what?'

'"System A". Or "SISTEMA". It's the bedrock of metaconsciousness that everything else is built on.'

'The Structure...'

He turned to me. 'What now?'

'The Structure. We call it "the Structure".'

'Ah. Okay. Two names for the same principle. As I was saying, since Vathos source code is built to run on System A, it should go without saying that the major flaw in its design is simply *that*, that effectively the source code *must* operate at root level, and were one so inclined…'

His hands danced on the keyboard like bees attending to the hive. I finished the sentence for him. '…one could hack Vathos bottom up, from the Structure.'

He turned and smiled. 'System A – the Structure – is the insertion point. We've already done it, albeit it was a rather patchy job. And I'm sure your security was all over it…'

I nodded.

'But what they probably fail to understand is security on their systems will never be foolproof, since System A always demands root access, so to speak.'

'That still doesn't change the fact that our security systems are designed to pick up any breach. We did the first time, we just didn't recognize your signals. Once you insert yourself into our mainframe, that's it – we got you. There's no disguising the intrusion.'

'Theoretically, yes…'

I shook my head. 'But?'

'Last time we inserted ourselves digitally into your systems. We thought we were being clever, and it was a good design – I built the program myself – and we evaded the firewalls, but we still left an imprint once we were inside the mainframe.'

'So what's different now?' I glanced up at Eric, who was watching me intently.

'Well, this time we're not gonna go in digitally. This time, we're gonna go in *cerebrally*.'

It took a minute to click. 'Wait… you wanna jump in through me?'

He grinned and winked. 'Exactly. We're gonna propel ourselves into your systems by effectively bootstrapping off your consciousness into the operating program and hence onto the Vathos servers—'

'Wait a minute – that would need some kind of terminal point… you wanna inject something into me?'

Verne shook his head. 'Not inject, no. It's a tiny implant, we can insert it right below the ear. It'll enable us to surf your consciousness, right onto the mainframe…'

The guy was fidgeting excitedly, unable to contain his passion.

I shook my head. 'We got scanners all over the place in there – going in, coming out. They'd pick it up, for sure.'

'It's completely organic,' Eric said, dropping to one knee and resting an arm on the desk behind Verne. 'Just like the epidurals, it's designed to biodegrade in a very short time. Completely undetectable.'

'And if the operation runs longer than it should, and the thing degrades while you're still poking around on the servers?'

Eric nodded slowly. 'We're against the clock. There's no getting around it. We'll do what we need to do and get out. No one is under any illusions that this will be a walk in the park. We know what we're up against, and we know the risks.'

I folded my arms and sighed. 'I'm hearing a lot of assumptions here. I mean, have you tested the software already?' I looked at Verne.

'We've run tests…'

'But not live.'

'Not live.'

'And what about the implant? Who's to say it doesn't trigger our detectors…'

Eric held out his hand and Verne opened a drawer, taking out a small sealed plastic bag. He handed it to Eric.

'We need to do a test run.'

I took a deep breath and sighed. 'Of course you do.'

'Are you willing?'

I shook my head. 'Sure – why the fuck not.'

'When are you in the office next?'

'I'm back in later today,' I said.

'Alright. You're gonna have to insert this yourself, which may be tricky. But I'll show you how.'

The car park was quiet when I pulled in, not that it was ever busy. Hours at Vathos were so staggered that people were coming and going at all hours of the day, which meant you very rarely saw the same face twice as you were getting into work.

I got out of the car and locked it. I was walking toward the elevator when the doors opened and Sura stepped out. She sighed, as if coming off a long and torturous shift.

'You look wrecked,' I said.

She rolled her eyes. 'Fuck you too.'

'Tough day?'

'As it goes, yeah. But I'm goin' home, and you ain't.' She grinned.

'Charming,' I said, as she breezed passed me. I heard her car alarm deactivate somewhere behind us.

'See ya…'

She didn't look back. I turned to the lift. The doors were still open. In an instant I calculated what would happen if I stepped into the lift and the system detected a foreign body in my system. Would an alarm go off? I'd no idea. To my knowledge it had never happened before. Likely the alarms would be triggered silently, and I'd be met at the Subversion floor by a couple of guys from Security, maybe Rodin himself, and escorted to a darkened room. After that, who's to say what'd happen.

I'd hung about long enough. I stepped into the lift, turned and pushed the button. The doors closed.

The elevator was silent. My heart wasn't. It thundered in my chest. Were they monitoring my bio-signs at this very moment? Fuck knows. All I knew was, if there was someone waiting for me at the lift when it opened, I was a dead man walking.

The lift opened and I was greeted by an empty hallway.

I stepped out of the lift on shaky legs, and made my way down the hall. I looked down at my hand. It was balled into a fist. I flexed it and let it fall to my side.

DP was in the canteen. He nodded as I came in.

'What's up man?' I said, going to the coffee machine. I turned it on.

'All good. You alright? You look kinda *peaky…*'

My hand went to the back of my ear. Noticing it, I folded my arms. 'I'm fine, dude. Fucking fine.'

8

Paranoia. Doesn't bother you if you're not doing anything that makes you look over your shoulder. Or on hard drugs. I could feel it clawing its way in. Not serious yet, but that's the way it starts. An itch. A niggling. A thorn. And when it gains a foothold, it begins to amplify. Until what started as a prick soon becomes a gash, becomes a gaping wound in your mind. Then you begin to trip up: second-guessing yourself, going over covered ground trying to spot your errors and telltale signs… I'd have to watch myself. Get on top of it or get out. The worst of it was, in my field there was a very thin line, almost nonexistent, between paranoia and a very dangerous, tangible reality that only had one exit.

Sleep never came easy. Less so now. I slept with the window open; the sound of the trees outside was background noise and helped silence the inner disquiet. Sleep, when it did come, didn't last long.

I snapped out of the uneasy slumber, grabbing the arm that held the knife to my throat. She stared at me with those eyes full of fire.

'Do you know the risk you're taking?' I said softly, the blade cutting into my throat right below the Adam's apple.

'I'm willing to risk everything to do what I need to do,' Celeste whispered.

'You can do nothing from the grave.'

'Are you gonna kill me?' she said, increasing the pressure on the blade.

I shook my head almost imperceptibly. 'No. But the people I work for will.' She never blinked, never took her eyes from me. I couldn't discern any trembling in her hand. 'Did you follow me home?'

She ignored the question. 'Are you leading us into a trap?'

'Do the others know you're here?'

She pressed down on the blade. 'Answer the question.'

I took a breath, my hand not letting off her arm. 'No.'

She tilted the blade so the point broke the skin, her eyes still boring into me. Then she relaxed the pressure, and straightened up.

'No, they don't. I'm here on my own.'

'You do a lot of crazy shit on your own, do you? What else have you been up to?' I dabbed the blood on my neck with a finger. 'Fuck sake. Couldn't have held the knife a little further up, huh? I could've passed it off as a shaving cut.' I turned to look at the open window. 'You know they've probably got you on some kind of file, don't you? You're probably under surveillance, and here you are, creeping through the window of one of their own. Lunatic.'

She looked at the kitchen knife in her hand as if she'd only suddenly become aware of it. I threw back the bed cover and stood up. I held out my hand.

'I take it you've decided not to stick that thing in me?' She handed me the knife and took a step back. 'My own knife, huh?'

I turned and dropped it on the bedside table.

'Is that you?' she said.

'Is what me?'

'On your back – the tattoo. Is that you?'

I shook my head. 'I dunno. I've never seen it.'

'Why are you helping us?'

I looked at her for a second. Then I walked past her, heading for the kitchen. 'I have no fucking idea.'

After I'd made coffee we sat down in the darkened living room. We were silent for some time and I listened to the dark whisper of the trees outside. Sometimes it was a balm. Sometimes they sang ill. Celeste looked around the house, eyes roving over every corner of my home. I waited for her to say something.

'Pays well, does it, what you do?' She turned to me with a jagged look.

'Look lady, I understand what you have against the people I work for – and me, for that matter – but you're the one that crept into my home and went at my throat with a blade. I might be asking just how much difference there is between you and the people you hate so much.'

'Don't you dare compare me with those people. *You*. I am not like you bastards and never will be.'

'And what – the ends justify the means, is that it? Stealing in here and threatening me with a knife? That's alright so long as it's for justice?'

'I would happily slit the throats of the men who killed my son, yes. That would be justice. Justice and cold-blooded murder are not the same thing. You do what you do for money, nothing else. I do what I do because I have to. Because no one else will. In a better world the men who murdered Caleb would have sat trial, and maybe even got the death penalty. But we don't live in that world. That's why I'm going after my own justice.'

'Nature red in tooth and claw…'

'You are the animals. Not us.'

I said nothing. She was probably right. Still, she'd threatened me in my own home. She was lucky to be alive. I told her so.

'Why didn't you kill me then?'

I sighed. 'I'm not a killer. That's not what I do.'

'And what were you in that restaurant for that night, if not to kill me? Right? You were supposed to do the job your friend did, right?'

I didn't reply. I could see I still disgusted her. There was part of her that didn't want to believe people like me and companies like Vathos existed. Yet incontrovertibly we did, and that upset her. She was no idealist, but perhaps she hoped we might live in a better world than we really did. I was proof we didn't. Maybe people like me were living proof of the banality of evil. Beneath her hatred, there was incomprehension.

Her silence gave me leave not to answer. Instead she hit me with the thing I was supposed to inflict on her that night in the restaurant, and which Maynes had done instead.

'You know that night, when that sick bastard killed me, you know what I felt right before he cut off my head? Relief. Pure exhilarating relief, that I no longer had to suffer this sick world. I mean, it was… beautiful. Like I was free, just for a moment. Then I died with the most horrific pain you can imagine.'

I nodded slowly. 'You'd be surprised the amount of pain I can imagine.'

She shook her head and looked at the floor. When she looked up, she said, 'I'm going into that program with only one object in mind – to ruin the people you work for. And yes, I might die trying, but I've died before, and dying wasn't the worst thing. I'll happily die again if I can make you people suffer.'

'You're not the only one who's lost someone,' I said.

'Fuck you. Don't you dare play the victim. You do not get to play the victim. There are those that have suffered, and there are those who sow misery. You will never be with us.'

I sighed and stood up. 'You sure have a way of asking for help. Maybe you should go before I change my mind and pick up that phone. I think you've said enough for one night.'

She stood.

'You gonna climb back out the window the way you came?'

'He was fourteen.'

I nodded, and lowered my eyes. 'Yeah. I know.'

She watched me for a few moments, then turned and walked through the kitchen toward the back door.

'I'll turn off the security lights for you, shall I?'

She opened the door, then turned to look at me. 'Will I see you in there, when they put me into the program?'

I shrugged. 'Hard to say. But you might.'

'Will you be different?'

'Different how? How you see me probably depends on what you think about me. So no. I'll probably still be an asshole.'

She opened the door and stepped out into the night.

'Hey, what's the tattoo like?' I said. 'On my back…'

She stopped and turned. 'It's horrific.'

The smell of disinfectant was heavy in the air. Roche ignored me as I lay there on the table, busying herself with the gun in her hand.

'An acquaintance was admiring your work,' I said, staring at a piece of paper stuck to the wall with some grinning Asian-style demon on it.

'You showed my work to someone?' she said absentmindedly.

'No, I didn't show it. They saw it. Unintended.'

She turned to me. 'Bad luck for you.'

'What are you talking about?'

'You show unfinished work to someone, it's bad luck. Shit will come down upon your head, and it's only yourself you have to blame.'

'Bullshit,' I said.

'You will see.'

She placed a hand on my back to still me. I heard the needle buzz, then she drove it into me close to the spine. My head shot up off the table.

'Jesus fucking Christ, what are you doing?'

She put a hand on my head and pushed it down. 'A reminder. Not to tempt fate. Now be still.'

When the work was done, she wiped down my back. She ran a hand over the work appreciatively.

'I think I wanna see it,' I said.

'I don't think you do.'

'I changed my mind. I wanna see it.'

She gripped the muscle of my shoulder tightly between thumb and forefinger and pinched.

'Agh, fuck – let go!'

'Stick to your promise. You said you wouldn't look. So don't. Only weak men change their mind.'

Before I could shrug her off, she let go.

'Fuck is wrong with you tonight?' I said.

'Go on, mention my period. I dare you.'

'I wasn't gonna say shit about your period.'

She turned away and popped the needle from the gun, wiped it down and put it into the sterilizer. I began to sit up.

'Don't move.' Silently, I lay back down. When she was done with her tools she put salve on the tat and dressed it. 'Now you may get up.'

'Jesus. Thanks.'

I got up and lifted my T-shirt.

'But don't get dressed.'

I looked at her and raised an eyebrow. 'One of those nights, is it?'

'Sit in the chair.'

I dropped the T-shirt and sat down, and sighed. When she looked at me with mild disdain, I had a sudden recollection. Or more like something clicked into place. I understood the dynamic. In my youth I'd been involved with all the wrong women, toxic relationships that corroded everything and drove you to the point of insanity, drove you to violence. This was no relationship, but sure as shit it replaced something I thought I'd said goodbye to long ago. Roche and I were no lovers, but the same dynamic persisted here. *Why did I ever fuck her?* I thought.

Then she turned, and I saw the regal curve of her back

through the backless top she was wearing, and all my resolve, my fortitude, drained away.

She came behind the chair and leaned over, sliding her hands down my arms and into my hands. Then she pulled my arms behind the chair and tied them together.

'Roche,' I said, 'I'm sure you're a hell of a lot of fun when you're playing dom, but look, I've gotta get going…'

She came around in front, leaned in and kissed me. Then she undid my belt and slid it from my pants.

'Jesus Christ, Roche…' She folded the belt. '…A quick fuck, mayb—'

Before I could react, she belted me across the chest with it, stunning me. When my shock passed, the burning sting set in.

'Roche, let me up outta this fucking chair…'

The back of her hand struck my cheek. 'Shut your mouth. Or I'll gag you.'

'I'm not in the mood, Roche—let me up outta the fuck—'

Again the hand struck my cheek. My face burning now.

'You don't know it, but this is just what you need right now. Shut your mouth and take it. You are not being a man tonight. Recognize what is happening, and accept it.'

She stood back, raising the belt. Then she brought it down across my torso with great force. I opened my mouth to shout, but no sound came out. A feeling of resignation came over me. I looked her in the eye with desire and hatred.

'Good. Now let me do what I need to do.' She raised the belt in the air.

It's the curse of this earth that the same women who know how to destroy a man are often those who know how to make him. And when I walked outta there, I felt fucking incredible.

9

'Who the hell's the kid?'

I looked at the boy. He couldn't have been more than fifteen years old. Eric put a hand on his shoulder.

'His name's Saleh. He was a friend of Celeste's boy. He's been training with us. He's gonna help us with the operation.'

'Are you kidding? You're gonna put a kid in there… do you realize how much is at stake?'

'He's good at what he does. Really good. He takes to System A like a duck to water, knows his way around it like you wouldn't believe. He can do things the rest of us can only imagine. He's our best asset, believe me.'

I took a deep breath. It was my job on the line, possibly my life. I said so.

Celeste spoke up. 'I can't do it alone. I can help Saleh get to the firewall, but only he can breach it. We tried it, many times. He's the one can slip through undetected. I can only get him there.'

I looked at the kid. 'That true? You know your way around the Structure?'

He nodded and shrugged. 'Yeah, it's pretty easy. You just gotta go with your gut.'

'With your gut, huh? You know anything about code, cybersecurity, machine learning?'

He shook his head. 'I don't know what that is.'

'We've trained Saleh in firewall response,' Eric said, tightening his grip on the kid's shoulder, 'all using programs built on Vathos source code. You need to trust me when we say he's got what it takes to punch through the walls. He's made of strong stuff. Tougher than he looks.'

'Yeah, he's also a kid. It's you that'll have it on your conscience if anything happens to him.'

'We're aware of that. And Saleh's aware of it too. He's not going in blind. He knows the risks.'

'I can't believe you sprung this on me at the last minute.' I shook my head. 'Probably because you knew I wouldn't go along with it.'

The boy stepped forward and held out his hand. 'I promise I won't let you down.'

I raised an eyebrow. 'Got balls at least, I'll give you that.' Reluctantly, I shook his hand. Didn't make me any more comfortable with the set-up.

'So… let's get down to brass tacks, shall we?' Eric turned and motioned to Verne, who opened a small box on the table in front of him and took out an implant, same as the one we'd already tested. He handed it to Eric, who handed it to me.

'It's ready to go. Now that we know it gets past the Vathos security systems, all we have to worry about is the 'hop' – jumping from your consciousness to—'

I held up a hand. 'You know I can't hear anything about what you're gonna do. Don't tell me anything. I don't wanna be going in there with some pre-printed recollections that'll upset the program.'

'I know that. I wasn't gonna reveal any details. Just know that we are well-prepared, and we've run through every conceivable permutation with Celeste and Saleh. There's nothing more can be done than we already have. I just want you to know that. We're aware of the risks you're taking, and they are not unappreciated.'

I looked at Celeste. Her face was blank, but her eyes still

spoke much rage. Her gaze was defiant. It told me the break-in at my house was entirely her own doing; no one else in the room was aware of what had happened. Deep down, no matter what I did, she'd always hate me, blame me for her son's death, even though I'd no part in it, nor had any knowledge of it.

I turned to the boy. 'You're looking for something else when you get onto the servers,' I said, folding my arms. 'Not just Vathos records – something for me.'

'Your sister.'

I nodded. 'You're not gonna forget, are you?'

He shook his head. 'No sir.'

Celeste put an arm around him. 'You don't need to call him "sir".'

I turned away, shaking my head. 'Right then – anything else? Anything we haven't gone over before I go and throw my job down the toilet and possibly get myself killed?'

Eric held out his hand. 'Like I said, we all owe you a debt. And our gratitude.'

I put my hands in my jacket pockets. 'Maybe best you save it for after.'

DP was in the operations room with Maynes. On the table in front of them was a laptop. I heard the quiet sound of background noise; they were patched into Sura's team as she led Analeptics to the target's house to prep for the op. I sat down quietly, Maynes's eyes darting to me briefly before returning to the screen. I glanced at DP; he nodded. I sat back in the chair and waited for the operation to take its course.

—We're moving, sir.

Sura, communicating with Coates. Subversion with a one-way audio feed. I didn't need to see the screen to know what was happening. Sura's team would be moving toward the mansion, crossing the fields in the direction of the target's house. And when they were in, they'd patch him into us. Then we'd go to work.

Maynes looked up from the computer. "Bout time you two were gettin' ready. Go and get set up. I'll patch you through to Sura when she's inside.'

'Sir.' DP stood up. I followed him out of the room and down the hall. He opened his mouth again when we were well out of earshot. 'Ready, killer?'

'I'm no killer, DP. Just a grunt like you.'

He hit me playfully on the arm. 'Don't be coy with me, fucko. We both know you got the instinct.'

Once inside the room, he dropped into his seat in front of the console and punched a few keys. 'Ready for the hunt?'

I sat down in the chair, hand going behind my ear. My fingers grazed the spot where the implant was embedded just under the dermis.

'I'm ready. Just put that crossbow in my hand. I'll nail him to the wall.'

He got up and applied the epidural, then gave me a light slap on the chest. 'Once more into the fray…'

I glanced up at him. 'What's that?'

'That right there is some poetic shit, partner, that you say to a buddy before he goes and turns shit upside down.'

'Is that right?'

'That is right.' He sat back down, putting on the headset.

I turned my head to glance at him. He was sitting side-on to me, eyes on the screen.

'We got a few minutes before Sura's ready to go. Want me to lay down a base operational overlay and put a crossbow in your hands, you can play about with it?'

'Sure,' I said.

He punched a few keys.

'Hey what's the second line to that poem you just said, DP? I think I know it from somewhere…'

'Huh? Oh – "Once more into the fray, Into the last good fight I'll ever know, To live and die on this day, To live and die on this day."'

'Huh.' I looked at the ceiling. 'Fucking epic.'

'You're the man, Zervas. You know that.'

'Hey DP…'

'What's that?'

'Screw you, partner.'

'Love you too man.'

He hit the key. I was blinded, and when I opened my eyes I was standing amongst the trees in the darkness. I looked down to see the hunter's crossbow in my hand. I raised it.

—What do you wanna hunt?

'Surprise me,' I said.

I knelt to the ground, bracing the crossbow against my hip. Shoulder against a tree, I peered out into the woods. I had a curious sense of the forest. As if it moved through me. I raised the bow, taking aim out into the dark, settling on the burr of an oak around thirty paces from me. I held a second, absolutely focused, before letting go the trigger. The arrow flew, speeding from the breech, then slowed, coming to an absolute standstill in the air, halfway between me and the oak.

—Looks good from here. Feel like chasing down some big game?

'You know what, DP, I'm not in the mood. Just leave me to enjoy the woods. I like it here like this. It's calming.'

—Hell's gotten into you?

'I feel a tremendous sense of peace. Let me savor it.'

—Do what the hell you like, partner. I'll shout you when we're ready.

The line went quiet. I stood up, moving out from behind the tree. I stood quietly listening to the woods. The trees spoke with a gentle whisper, a voice we will never understand but which speaks worlds. There was some kind of sphericality to the way I was embedded in the program, like it enveloped me, encircled me and gravitated around my being. Nothing moved, of course, but that's how it felt. I was at the center: the cause and the cessation. And it made me feel oddly tranquil.

I reached down to put a hand on the ground. It was warm to the touch. Earthy. When I stood up again, I began to walk in what I sensed was in the direction of the target's house. Moving on instinct. Even though the operation hadn't begun, the overlay was the same. Same terrain. I heard an owl and paused, and listened to the echo of that ominous howl in the night, a portentous lament of the nightwatcher. *Speak, seer. What is it that awaits?*

The howl had nothing to tell me, nothing it could relate in a language I could understand, only rippling ululations that disturbed the forest's silent clamor.

By quiet footfall I moved. None would hear me come. *I go silently, in your dreams I appear and render sinister. I am the one you do not hear.*

I reached the treeline and paused, looking out from the woods to see the shadow of a building, what I took for the barn. I was behind the estate. Feeling the need to scan the area, I threw the crossbow on my back and leapt onto the tree, scaling the trunk in a matter of seconds, perching myself on a sturdy limb to look out over the barn to the parapet of the house beyond. A single tower that rose up from the north flank. The window in the tower aglow with light, dimmed by a pair of burgundy curtains. Beyond it, dreams being dreamed, those dreams a dream within a dream, from which nightmares would arise. I raised the scope of the bow to my eye to better see the window. Behind it nothing moved. I lowered the bow onto my knee and looked out over the ground between the tree and the mansion. It occurred to me that my presence there was like an infection: a virus penetrating the mind of the unwary to bring only harm. And with me this time, an entirely novel bacteria, one that had no place in that environment and which had come with the intention of infecting the system. Right at that moment, Celeste and Saleh were getting ready to propel into the program using my consciousness to bootstrap in. Were they here already? Lurking in the dark, watching? I had invited them. No good would come of it, that was for sure. What happened from here on in, I couldn't predict. And yet I felt safe.

—Ready?

'Sura's in?'

—Epidural's just been applied. I'm patching you into operational.

The forest shuddered, the scene before me evaporating and reconstituting in an instant. The operation was live. I leapt down from the tree, landing on the ground below. I felt the ground rise to meet me, then my feet sink into the soft earth, the ground rapidly righting itself so that I was stable on two feet. I stood, raising the crossbow to my chest.

—Sura has injected the deliriant. Shouldn't be long now.

'What if he doesn't come out?' I said.

—Just trust in Analytics, partner. They know the score.

I nodded. 'Alright then.'

I moved toward the barn, coming to rest by the wall, going down on my hunkers. A movement to my left, just on the edge of the treeline, caught my eye. My heart stopped.

—Fuck was that? DP said, a frantic edge in his voice.

'You see something?' I shifted nervously.

—Yeah… thought I just saw a fucking kid.

I thought I had too. Didn't say it though. 'Maybe it was a wolf, DP. You messin' around with me?'

—In the middle of an operation? You gotta be kidding.

'Wouldn't be the first time.'

There was a moment's silence. I moved from behind the barn, stealing across the grass to an old plow that lay like a rusted skeleton in the middle of the yard. I knelt by the wheel.

—Dude, Sura's team have just left. We're at the mercy of the numbers now, partner. All you do is wait for that door to open. I'm goin' silent. Gonna run that segment again, see if it was just a glitch.

'Sure thing. See ya.'

—Good luck.

DP logged off. I sighed tensely. Didn't like company when I was in operations, never had. And now the knowledge that there were two intruders in the Vathos operational network was clawing at me. There was nothing to do but get on with the operation and hope they didn't trigger any alarms. Nothing like this had been done before.

I watched the entrance to the kitchen of the house, where it was predicted the target would flee from. My heart was racing. I calmed it with controlled breathing. There were more stresses now than I normally carried into an operation. Baggage. Always baggage of some kind.

I heard something from inside, a thump, as if something had just crashed into the door. Moments later, it flew open, and a man stumbled out wrapped in a black silk robe and with a white hood on his head. He was howling like a banshee, voice torn with terror. He fell to his hands and knees, scrambling on the ground, then got up and ran blindly across the yard. Possessed by some kind of feral lust, I howled like a wolf. The fleeing figure jerked his neck at the sound, causing him to stumble and fall again. I watched him scrabble around, rising to his feet only to tumble again and race over the ground on all fours like an animal.

I followed, keeping distance. I could almost smell his fear, except it wasn't a smell – it was more like a taste in my mouth, a metallic tang, a satisfying bitterness. I knew already who'd win the battle, but the thrill of the hunt was no less pronounced. There would be blood.

I followed the raving figure across the front lawn and watched him flee down the steps into the parterre garden. Where I'd passed in the training exercise. I decided to shoot off an arrow, to juice things up a little. I paused by the sculpted hedge under cover of dark night and fell to one knee. Elbow poised on my thigh, I took aim at the fleeing figure and sent fly an arrow clean into the back of his right calf. He screamed and fell to the ground, crawling forward desperately, before struggling to his feet and dragging himself toward the woods.

I descended the steps into the garden, howling once more. The metallic taste in my mouth getting stronger, my limbs bristling with a kind of animal hunger. The woods beckoning. The quarry fleeing right into the heart of darkness. It was no hunt, after all, but merely a long and drawn-out torture. I had expected more. This little charade was practically over already.

I watched the figure crawl into the trees, the white hood on his head marking him clearly against the backdrop of the forest. There was nowhere he could run I wouldn't find him. Better to put an end to it quick and be done with it. I tapped my ear to alert DP, to ask him to run the numbers by Analytics.

'DP?'

No answer. I tried again with the same result. Having no other option, I followed the target into the woods, trying one final time as I entered the trees.

'DP?'

Nothing. I stepped over a fallen trunk, watching the quarry scurry amid the shrubbery. I followed, slowly and deliberately. Quietly. Then, raising the crossbow, I fired, striking him in the left thigh. More screams. He disappeared behind the trunk of a huge redwood as I followed his every step.

Something in the air changed. An electricity, or a charge. Like the trees stopped whispering and fell silent. I felt the pull of a tremendous gravity, like that of a dying star.

Stepping out from behind the redwood into a clearing, I saw the figure in the black silk gown crawl to the edge of an enormous swirling black hole in the ground. He rolled onto his back and began to howl with laughter. *Something in that laughter…*

I raised my crossbow as I stepped into the clearing, staying well away from the hole. I felt it pull at me, draw me closer. It was a struggle to resist.

I raised the crossbow at the prostrate figure. 'Take off your hood,' I said, not stepping closer.

The figure continued to laugh.

'Take off the fucking hood.'

He raised a hand and took hold of the hood, wrenching it up over his head. Raising his face to me, he grinned.

'Maynes…?'

'You imbecile… how long did you think you could get away with it, huh? What made you think you could fuck over the company and get out alive?'

I stared at him, mouth open.

'You're a dead man. You know that, don't you?' He sat up, then stood, arrows still protruding from his limbs, the silk of the black gown shiny with blood. He raised his hand from under the gown. In it was a gun. Instinctively I raised my hands to take aim, but the crossbow was no longer in my hand.

'Asshole. We control the Structure. We say what comes in. And you're lucky we haven't put a bullet in your head already.'

'Then why the fuck waste my time letting me play like I'm still on operations. What am I doing here?'

He glanced at the hole in the ground and smiled. 'Because you're a guinea pig, Zervas. You're goin' in there. And you're not gonna like what you find there. But we just wanna see how you take it. And if you do come out, we'll put a bullet in your head all the same.'

'What's in the hole?' I said.

He grinned. Then his face went cold. 'Hell. Hell is in there.'

I shook my head. 'I'm not goin' in there. You can shoot me, but I am not jumping in that fucking hole.'

'Oh yes you are.'

I glanced at the ground, looking for a rock or something.

'Don't even think it. You're not getting out of this one, you traitorous piece of shit. You're finished.'

A shot rang out, and I saw Maynes double over, the gun dropping from his hand. I looked around frantically; Celeste stepped from the trees, gun raised and pointed.

Maynes looked up, blood pouring from his shoulder. He

stared at her for a second, before his eyes widened in shock.

'You…'

Celeste's eyes brimmed with rage. Fear too. 'Yeah, you remember me, don't you…'

'Fuck are you doing here?' He looked from her to me, uncomprehending. 'Huh? I fucking killed you…'

'Yeah, you did…' She stepped forward, putting another bullet in him. Maynes stumbled back. 'You killed me and raped me, you sick piece of shit.' Another round screamed in the night. Maynes stumbled back, blood erupting from his stomach. 'And now I'm going to kill you.'

Two more shots. Before she could squeeze off a third, some black demon-like animal bounded from the trees and lunged, coming to land on her back and sending her careening toward the hole. I shouted, reaching out, but the sound of her scream was already receding downward as I watched her disappear.

I looked up, seeing Maynes reach for the gun at his feet. I ran and threw myself at him. Locked at each other's throats, we tumbled into the swirling void.

*

Saleh eyed the steps that led to the basement door of the mansion from behind the shed. The way across the yard was clear. It was the howling that gave him pause – was he in danger of attack? The wolf he imagined twice his size, teeth like knives and eyes that shone with menace.

He'd been into SISTEMA many times and knew the tricks it could play. He pushed the terrifying thoughts to the back of his mind, his fingers pinching the corner of the building that he clung to. He recalled the plan. Knew there was only one way in. Through the basement door, a back door that had been reprogrammed to give access to Vathos's servers.

Steeling himself, he dashed from behind the shed and ran across the yard, and down the steps. Panting, he paused to catch his breath, before looking up at the keypad on the door.

He lifted his hand to read the number scrawled on his palm:
1149. Holding his breath, he punched it into the keypad with
a shaking hand. When it clicked open, he exhaled and closed
his eyes. Then he pushed open the door.

Inside the door sat a man at a decrepit desk. Legs crossed,
he looked up at Saleh with a bored and disinterested look on
his face. He took a puff of his cigarette in an effete manner,
the ash dropping onto his stained yellow suit. He reached out
with his stained fingers, still with the cigarette between them,
and prodded the paper on the desk in front of him with a
finger.

'Sign here, if you'd pass,' he said, raising the cigarette to his
mouth again.

'Do I have to?' the boy said.

'All who would enter must sign.'

He eyed the boy, chin perched on his palm, smoke rising in
wisps around his thin face. The boy picked up the pencil and
scratched his name on the paper. When he put the pencil back
on the table, the man grinned, and with a theatrical flourish,
bade Saleh pass through.

'Make sure and say hello to your dead mother,' the man
said, taking the cigarette between his teeth.

Saleh looked at him once, eyes narrowed, before turning
and opening the door.

CONTINUE WITH PART FOUR...

1. Cerebrum

Subconscious torture for political and corporate subversion. That's the trade of Vathos—creeping into a target's dreams to force the shady ends of their clients. It's dirty business.

Vangelis Zervas is one of their Subversion agents and makes a living inflicting pain on people in their sleep. A recipient of the most stringent training and a man of few qualms, he'll do whatever it takes to get the job done. But when a series of events calls his dedication into question, strange things begin to happen when he infiltrates the dreams of his targets. Soon he's asking himself—is it he in the mark's head, or is someone else in his?

A no-holds-barred dystopian horror that will put your teeth on edge.

2. Acolyte

Caleb, a young school dropout, robs an apartment one night with his petty-criminal friend, Vince. Finding an expensive and rare piece of computer hardware, he pockets it, oblivious to its power and purpose. The boy plugs himself into the new device, unaware that the program inside it is a diabolical piece of software, one which almost kills him. But those who created the program do not want it out in the world and will do anything to retrieve it, including killing anyone in whose possession it is found. Caleb may find that by taking the device he has unwittingly unleashed forces that will consume all he knows and loves.

3. Chimera

Following the murder of her young son, Celeste goes all in with a group of co-conspirators to infiltrate Vathos, the company she believes responsible for the death of her child. The faction make tentative contact with Vangelis Zervas, hoping he will help them penetrate the Vathos servers so they may gather evidence to bring the company down. Despite the nature of his ruthless and horrific work, Vangelis may have his own misgivings with the company. But is it enough for him to turn on Vathos?

In the end, he may have only one choice: Hell or death.

4. Inferno

After a penetration operation on the Vathos servers goes awry, Celeste and Vangelis Zervas are cast into the Vathos mainframe following a possible sabotage operation from within the company. The pair are drawn into the 'Inferno' program, a devious piece of software long held in the companies archives, the program a digitalized recreation of Hell itself. Celeste and Zervas are pursued by Maynes, who, having discovered that the agent has gone rogue, is hell-bent on retribution. But no one gets through Inferno unscathed. Evil begets evil, and soon Celeste and Zervas will come face to face with something far darker, and far more sinister than Maynes.

5. Diablo

Within every man is a devil. There is only one Satan.

Vangelis Zervas has just been subjected to the most insidious psychological program ever invented by man. He comes out of it in a coma, sequestered in the Medical wing at Vathos systems. Maddox Maynes, his supervising officer, has also returned from their encounter in 'Inferno', still conscious but carrying something deeply sinister within him. The reverberations of the program are carried from the virtual into the real, as Vathos is shaken from within by the greatest enemy it will ever face. This is the beginning of the end.

LITTLE SWINE

A small basement cell. A dirty bed. A chair.

These are the confines of Little Swine's world. Prisoner of Momma and subject to the tortures of Boy, her life is a living hell.

Momma has a plan. Momma wants a baby that she may redeem the sins of her past. This is Little Swine's purpose. And when Momma has what she wants, Little Swine will be discarded.

But violence begets violence and blood begets blood, and many will die before the devil has his quota. One can never underestimate the power of retribution.

THE COTTAGE

Men are men until they encounter evil. And after, they are compelled to do evil itself.

Turning their backs on New York, John and Katie Mears purchase their dream home in colonial Connecticut, the place they hope to raise their firstborn and build life as a family. But the cradle of the American nation has a haunting past, and they find themselves swallowed by a dark history, one of blood and anguish, a specter of the country's painful birth in the slaughter of pilgrim times. The dark crucible of the nation is yet manifest. Blood debt is eternal, and sooner or later history calls for retribution. It is the blood of innocents that pays for the sins of the father.

MEAT

In the murky wake of the financial crisis a string of establishments pop up across Europe catering to a hedonistic underground, its clientele beholden to a strange, hallucinatory meat. Stoked by the fleshy and charismatic Hugo and fuelled by voracious consumption of ecstasy, the craze spreads from the heart of Europe all the way to the Mediterranean, where in Athens the financial elite begin to turn on each other. Murder, barbecue and apocalyptic raving ensues, culminating in the most savage party Mykonos has ever seen. Follow the story to its destructive end, where consumption eats itself alive.

NOTES FROM A CANNIBALIST

1847. Assuming the identity of a dead Jesuit priest, a survivor of the famine in Ireland travels to South America where he is tasked with rebuilding the missions among the natives. Inducted into local life, Father James Carmichael finds love with a native woman and becomes acquainted with the ways of the Guaraní, discovering ayahuasca and ritualism. In a battle with his own gods and demons, the priest fights for the life he envisions, his own self the ultimate stake of the struggle. Worlds are shattered, realities crumbled, lives destroyed. His soul victim to the crucible of the New World, what is tempered in the chaos will be outside his control.

A WHORE'S SONG

Hidden away in the backstreets of Amsterdam is a secretive whorehouse, open only to those in the know, where torture, pain and extreme sexual sport are the vehicle to understanding and self-knowledge. Run by the obscure Madame Zhu, the establishment is a magnet to the city's elite and mad soul-seekers alike. Two lives collide in a chaotic downward spiral brought about by psychoactives and sexual torture when, over the course of a day, a whore recounts her life as a destroyer of egos and one man is forced to face his deepest demons. Cast out into the far reaches of his mind, will he make it back from the other side?

In a world where the weak become prey and strength means brutality, living may come at the cost of dying first.

The Book of God

God isn't dead. He's just a bit mental...

Indignant at his corrupt and ignominious creation, God sits and stews in his treehouse outside the small town of Brawl. His only companion and sole remaining attendant, a withered and tortured scribe, chronicles the Lord's descent into madness as he struggles to collect all the lost souls which have escaped his records and further addled the Lord's already woolly mind. But when the Scribe is forced to hire a maid to care for the Almighty, the introduction of a buxom woman into God's life brings chaos in its wake. And what's more, the maid has an innocent and attractive young daughter...

Suffering rejection, humiliation and loathing of humankind, God seeks a way to bring back Christ and trigger the Apocalypse. The only thing standing in his way? God's old harpy of a mother...

The Jaguar

1849. Salome Azul, daughter of a powerful politician, flees Buenos Aires at the height of the Argentinian civil war. In London she enlists the help of Irishman Sean Ryan to open The Nightingale, a high-class brothel and opium den that will be used to entrap and blackmail London's political elite.

In doing so she will make enemies. What's more, Ms. Azul has carried her own demons from Argentina, and it is these that will prove her most relentless foe. In order to survive, she must eliminate all weakness from her character. Doing so may mean cutting away all she cherishes most.

In the pursuit of power, unrelenting sacrifice is what decides who lives and dies.

WORKS OF TRANSLATION BY ULTAN BANAN

Pietro Aretino's Dialogues

Nanna has been a nun. She's been a wife. She has also been a courtesan. And now, as her daughter turns sixteen, she must decide how to advise on her path in life. On what route should she send young Pippa?

Bawdy, filthy, hilarious and uproarious, listen to Nanna regale her friend Antonia with scandalous tales—tales of seduction, blasphemy, lies, dishonesty, thievery, nastiness, cruelty and treachery—in an attempt to decide on what course to set her daughter: should she be a nun, a wife or a whore?

ABOUT THE AUTHOR

Ultan Banan started writing as a way of getting his head straight, discovering in the process that staying busy is the only way to stop oneself going insane. He devotes what time he can to writing, doing his best to avoid gainful employment by increasingly creative means. He lives on the move but dreams of a small cottage on a foul and inhospitable coast somewhere. Currently in Scotland.

Latest news at
ultanbanan.com

Substack:
ultanbanan.substack.com

Twitter:
twitter.com/ultanbanan

www.ingramcontent.com/pod-product-compliance
Lightning Source LLC
Chambersburg PA
CBHW032021180726
48283CB00008B/2781